DARK WATER

BARRY NAPIER

+ KEYLIGHT
BOOKS
AN IMPRINT
OF TURNER
PUBLISHING

Keylight Books
An imprint of Turner Publishing Company
Nashville, Tennessee
www.turnerpublishing.com

Dark Water: A Cooper M. Reid Supernatural Thriller

Cover design: Hannah Linder
www.hannahlinderdesigns.com

9798990024007 Paperback

Printed in the United States of America

"I got no future. I know my days are few. The present's not that pleasant, just a lot of things to do. I thought the past would last me but the darkness got that too."

~ Leonard Cohen

ONE

I t was the third time in a month that Jenny had woken up to
the sound of a child's laughter. Had her own child been
alive, this would have made sense. There were times when she
heard the noise and dared to imagine that the last four years had
only been a dream—that Henry was still alive.

But Henry was dead. He had drowned less than ten feet
away from the beach. They'd had a funeral and memorial service
without a body two weeks later.

By the time Jenny sat up in bed and her sleep-fogged mind
came around, she understood that a laughing child in her house
made no sense. Hearing it in the dead of night, and then remem-
bering that Henry was dead, created a sharp fear within her that
took her breath away. It was almost like he had died all over
again, and the anticipation of grief that was to come was too
much to comprehend.

But then she came fully awake and recognized the noise for
what it was. And it was definitely not Henry's laughter.

She'd heard the noise more than a dozen times in the last
year and had tried her best to ignore it. But this was the third
time within a week. It was becoming far too much to take.

"Sam," she said, nudging her husband. "You awake?"

"Yeah."

"Did you hear it?"

"I was trying to pretend I didn't."

That said, Sam sat up in bed next to her and cut on his bedside lamp. His hair was in disarray and he squinted against the light. It hurt Jenny to be reminded just how much Henry had taken after his father. Sometimes the resemblance was so uncanny that she felt like Henry might have actually taken up residence in Sam when he had left this world.

"It sounded like a girl this time," Jenny said.

"Yeah," Sam said, still trying to drag himself out of sleep.

Jenny didn't know how Sam could remotely think of sleeping after hearing what she had heard. A child's laughter, of course, was always cheerful and melodic. But when heard at two in the morning in a house that had not harbored a child in four years, it was menacing and creepy.

"Come on, then," Sam said groggily. "Let's go take a look."

"Aren't you scared?"

"Of course I am. That's why I want you to come with me."

Sam slid out of bed, dressed only in a pair of boxer briefs. He shoved his feet into his slippers and walked to the bedroom door.

He turned back to Jenny, and she saw that he was doing his best to stay calm. Underneath his façade of aloofness and tired annoyance, he was just as scared as she was. She assumed his attempt at indifference was his way of trying to assume the role of protector. She loved him for it, but he was doing a poor job.

"You can stay here if you want," he said.

She shook her head as she got out of bed and joined him. They stood by the bedroom door for a moment, trying to find the courage to go out. They had never actually seen anything or found anything out of place after hearing the laughter, so Jenny wasn't too scared. But the fact that they were actually *looking* for what she was beginning to think was a legitimate ghost or disembodied voice was frightening enough.

Sam took the lead and walked out into the hallway, cutting on the light. Jenny reached out and took his hand as they made their way down the hall. The house was quiet, the only sound coming from the murmur of waves crashing on the beach two hundred yards away. It was a sound they had long ago gotten used to—one that Jenny only ever heard distinctly when she was having trouble going to sleep.

"Any idea where it came from?" Sam asked her.

"Not sure. Maybe the dining room."

They walked down the hall, passing Jenny's study and the room that they were now calling the guest room but, at one time, had been Henry's bedroom. The door was closed and Jenny reached out to touch it. It was a habit she had started the day after Henry's death. She did it almost habitually whenever she walked down the hall.

The hallway led them to the large open living room and the adjoined kitchen, separated by a bar containing a wine rack, the day's mail, and a clear vase filled with seashells. When Sam cut on the lights, there was a moment when Jenny saw the darkened shape of a small person. But as her eyes adjusted, she saw the outline of the vase on the kitchen counter for what it was and allowed herself a moment to feel embarrassed.

She'd nearly screamed there for a moment.

The dining room sat off to the right of the kitchen and couldn't be fully seen until they were halfway across the living room. They walked across the living room, through the kitchen, and into the dining room. Jenny noticed that Sam was a bit quicker to cut the lights on now, slapping at the switch on the wall in a minor panic.

The dining room was just as empty as the rest of the house. The blinds on the sliding glass door leading outside were partially open, showing only the darkness outside. Jenny peeked out of them and saw the night-shrouded back porch and the beach beyond. She could barely see the ocean from where she stood, the white tips of waves meandering in the darkness.

She cut the porch light on and drew the blinds fully open. The porch was empty, as was the beach and the thin concrete walkway that ran from the back porch to the edge of their yard.

She slowly closed the blinds and turned to Sam. He was looking back into the kitchen, slowly turning in a semi-circle. He was rubbing at his messy hair as a frustrated look passed over his face.

"You okay?" Jenny asked.

"Yeah. But this is just getting old. We need to get some answers for this. If it's pranksters, we need to have them stopped. If it's…well, if it's *ghosts*, then we need to find out if there is anything we can do."

"We had those guys come in," Jenny reminded him shyly, knowing it was a sore point.

"Ah yes, the ghost hunters. And they didn't find anything. Remember?"

"I know. But still, I—"

Something shattered behind them.

Jenny let out a shriek of surprise and looked to the right. In the kitchen, the vase with the seashells had fallen from the bar and smashed on the floor. Glass shards and seashells were strewn cross the kitchen floor, the fragments of the vase twinkling in the glow of the overhead lights.

Neither of them said anything. They simply shared a look that communicated a single thought in that almost telepathic way that most married couples are able to do. The thought they shared was: *the vase was sitting in the middle of the bar; it didn't just fall off. It was pushed or thrown.*

Jenny crept closer towards Sam and took his arm. She was beginning to tremble as she looked at the mess. She felt tears coming on and wasn't quite sure why. When they had heard the laughter on other nights, it was always a boy. On each and every occasion, she'd wondered if it was Henry coming back to visit them just to make sure they were doing okay. Maybe to make sure they hadn't left their home by the beach just because he'd died there. Jenny wondered if her urge to cry was based on that —on wondering if Henry *had* been here at some point.

But the laughter had been distinctly girlish tonight.

And apparently, the little girl had not been a fan of their vase of seashells.

"Go back to bed," Sam said, his voice shaky. "I'll clean this up."

His eyes were distant and his face looked flushed.

"Not right now," Jenny said. "Sam...let's get out of here. We can grab a room at a hotel or something. I just can't—"

A high-pitched laugh filled the kitchen, a sound of pure joy. It had come from no more than six feet away from her.

Jenny screamed and put her hands to her mouth. She started to cry, realizing that the moment she'd heard the laughter, the entire house seemed to go cold. As she took a series of hitching breaths, another noise filled the kitchen and then the dining room. It sounded like the shuffling of running footsteps. They were moving so quickly that she wasn't sure how many pairs of feet she was hearing. Two...maybe three. It was hard to know for sure.

"Oh my God," Sam said, looking into the dining room and placing his arm tightly around Jenny's shoulder. He drew her closer, as if to protect her.

Jenny didn't want to turn around. She didn't want to see whatever it was that Sam was seeing. But she couldn't resist. Morbid human curiosity forced her to turn back toward the dining room.

She began to whimper when she saw small wet footprints on the carpet.

The prints led to the sliding glass door and out onto the back

porch, passing right through the glass. Crying now, Jenny went
to the door and looked out. The footprints were clearly visible on
their porch, too. They led down the stairs and into the yard
where they faded out to nothing, headed towards the dark and
endless sea beyond...in the direction of the place her son had
died.

TWO

Of all the places he had expected to end up after everything that happened to him, the beach was certainly not one of them.

When Cooper placed his bare feet into the sand, it felt like he had stepped into another world. While he wasn't necessarily trying to escape his past, he was definitely trying to hide from it for a while. Feeling the sand beneath his toes as he stared out to the ocean, he was pretty sure he was succeeding.

Cooper M. Reid had come to the beach quite a lot as a child. Until the age of fourteen, his family's traditional summer vacation had been a trip to Orlando. They would spend two days at the beach and two days at whichever Disney park he and his brother could agree on. And while that part of his life seemed like nothing more than a series of pleasant dreams during a deep and reviving sleep, he tried to focus on them as he watched the ocean.

Yet his mind wanted to go elsewhere. It wanted to remind him for the hundredth time that his more recent past was bound to catch up with him. He'd have people to answer to and he could potentially be in a lot of trouble.

He walked out to the edge of the water and let it slip over his toes. It was only the beginning of May and the water still had a cold bite to it. He watched a few gulls circling overhead and then peered further down the beach where a couple was walking hand in hand. This stretch of Kill Devil Hills, North Carolina, would be packed in two weeks or so, according to the bit of research he had done before visiting. But for now, it was mostly empty.

Cooper checked his watch and smiled. He had a meeting in half an hour, one that he had been waiting quite some time to have. How long he had been waiting, he wasn't quite sure. Time had become a very tenuous and perplexing concept to him over the last few months.

All he knew was that he hadn't spoken to anyone about the task he had in mind or, for that matter, why he had decided to run away from his very specific troubles. Knowing that he could verbally remove that weight through a simple conversation was incredible, but also terrifying.

Talking about the last few months was going to be hard. He hadn't spoken much of it out loud yet and he honestly wasn't sure if he was ready for it. But it had to be done if he wanted to move on—if he wanted answers.

Giving the ocean one last look, Cooper walked back up the beach toward the tiny dunes, and the wooden stairs and walkway that snaked through them. Beyond those dunes and stairs was the parking lot of the motel where he was staying. He slid his shoes back on when he reached the wooden walkway and headed to his car.

He felt like there were eyes on him as he started the engine and pulled out into the thin flow of pre-summer beach traffic. He knew it was silly, but he also knew that, in trying to escape the people that were no doubt looking for him, it was a feeling that he was going to have to get used to.

SHE WAS SITTING at a table by the edge of the pier, looking out onto a curved portion of beach filled with hotels. A small basket of what appeared to be popcorn shrimp sat in front of her. She was popping one into her mouth just as Cooper spotted her. She was wearing a basic halter top with jeans and a pair of cheap flip flops. Her eyes were hidden by her gold-tinted Aviators and her blonde hair was pulled back into a tight ponytail.

When she saw Cooper approaching, she smiled and took off her sunglasses. Her eyes grew brighter as her smile expanded. Cooper had forgotten how gorgeous she was, how radiant her smile could be, and how her eyes sparkled.

He was just glad to see her smiling as she stood up from the table and opened her arms for a hug. Cooper had worried that she might slap him hard across the face when they met. She'd have every right to do so, that was for sure.

Cooper met her quickly, filling her arms and returning the embrace. She smelled like suntan lotion and strawberries. The simple feel of her bobbing ponytail on his hand made Cooper feel like he was floating. It wasn't just that it was her, that it was Stephanie; it was the fact that it was the first physical contact he'd had with anyone in almost five months.

"I've missed you, Steph," Cooper said.

"You too," she replied.

Cooper could tell that she was close to tears and he didn't want to see her cry. He broke the hug as gently as he could and held her at arm's length. Being this close to her and looking directly at her face made him want to kiss her very badly. But they were different people now and time had done some strange things to both of them.

"Sit down, sit down," Stephanie said. "I'm not *even* trying to get sentimental today."

"Probably for the best," Cooper said.

He took his seat and looked out to the sea again. With Stephanie Pagent sitting across from him, and the beach behind them, Cooper felt like this might be what people meant when they referred to *paradise*. He couldn't remember the last time he had felt this happy—this *free*.

Of course, the conversation they needed to have would derail all of that. They sat in silence for a moment, taking each other in. A waiter came by, sneaking up on them from the bar that sat on the backside of the pier. Cooper ordered a beer and fish tacos, and then he and Stephanie returned to their silence.

As had always been the case, it was Stephanie that broke the quiet. And when she did, she did so with her usual intense focus, looking him in the eyes with the rapt attention that he had never been able to give her in return.

"It's been twenty months, Cooper," she said. "Almost two years. That's a long time."

"I know."

"Do you?"

"I do. Believe me. And one of these days, I'll tell you why it's been so long. I'll tell you everything. But I can't do that right now."

She nodded, as if this was exactly what she'd expected.

"You know," she said, "I thought you were dead for a while. When three months passed and I hadn't heard from you, I called your parents. They told me that they were assuming the same thing. They said the people you worked for had no answers for them. So me, your parents, and God knows who else...we all just assumed you were dead. Maybe the government finally put a bullet in your head to shut you up or something even worse had happened. I had no idea. I spent over a year thinking you had died."

"I know. I'm sorry."

"Do you know what it feels like to get a phone call from someone you had assumed was dead?" Stephanie asked.

"I can't say that I do."

"Well, it's freaking weird, okay?"

"I'm sure it i—"

"And now you want me keeping secrets, is that right?" she

interrupted. "I'm not clear on why you aren't telling your parents you're alive. Do you know how messed up that is?"

"I'm sorry, Steph," he said again. "But it has to be this way for now. You were the only one I thought would be able to help me *and* keep some secrets for a while."

"How long is *a while*?"

"I'm not sure yet."

She frowned and then, rather suddenly, said: "Oh!"

"What?"

She gave a sarcastic smile that Cooper enjoyed a little too much. "I almost forgot…"

She reached down beneath her seat and put her purse on the table. She pulled a trade paperback out and placed it on the opposite side of her basket of shrimp.

"Because most of the world assumes you're dead, do you have any idea what this goes for these days?" Stephanie asked.

Cooper looked at the book and felt his heart deflate. The title was very familiar. *Grasping the Fringes*. The name of the author was even more familiar: Cooper M. Reid.

"How much?" he asked.

"About five hundred bucks. Autographed copies fetch around three grand. I'm not going to lie to you…I sold mine."

"I don't blame you."

"The History Channel even did a special on you. *Spooky Smarts*, they called it."

"Seriously? That's…that's awful."

She nodded, selecting another shrimp and tossing it into her mouth. "I'm pretty sure you can watch it for free on YouTube."

"I think I'll pass."

She shrugged. "It was pretty good. They painted you as a pretty smart guy."

Cooper wasn't sure how to feel about that. A year or so ago, he would have probably been elated. But now it felt like he was dead and buried, yet alive at the same time, fully aware that people were egging his tombstone six feet overhead.

He looked back down to the book and frowned.

When he'd had the book published, it had been one of the happiest days of his life. But now it was a reminder of a life that he had not used to its full potential. Of course, that had been before he had gone missing for three months.

The things that had happened to him and the things he had seen—they all made the former Cooper, the one with the huge ambition and drive, seem like a careless fool. Oddly enough, though, he couldn't remember the things he had seen or what had happened to him. And that was the hardest part of all.

"Cooper...it *is* nice to see you," Stephanie said. "I can't even begin to explain how nice it is. And I want to help you in any way that I can. But I don't know that I'm going to be able to do anything illegal just to keep you a secret. If you have people in powerful places looking for you like you say, then how do you know they aren't watching us right now?"

"I've been extremely careful," Cooper said. "Before I made the decision to come here, I reached out to the only other friend I ever had. It's a guy I used to work with...someone I knew I could trust. He's kind of like you. He's a whiz with computers and spent some of his youth with hacker groups. Much like you, he's revered in paranoid online circles. He and I spent about three weeks making sure the people that I used to work with have no idea I'm back."

"How long *have* you been back?"

"Five months," Cooper said.

"All of the news reports said you disappeared while doing research for some weird case in Kansas. Is that right?"

"Close enough. But like I said...I'll tell you everything some other time. I just don't know that I can get through it all right now."

She gave him a look that was partly playful but mostly hurt. "So, for right now, you just need me to do some pretty sketchy favors for you, is that it?"

"Yeah," he said softly.

"And will you expect me to just come running whenever you ask?"

"Steph...it's not like that. Really."

Stephanie put her sunglasses back on. Cooper wasn't sure if this was some sort of defense mechanism or what. He had never been particularly good at reading women.

The waiter came back with Cooper's beer and tacos. Stephanie watched the waiter go, waiting for him to be out of earshot before she spoke.

"Well, I've already done some of the favors," she said. "The money, for instance. That's taken care of. And I have the address you asked for."

Again, she reached into her purse. This time she took out a plain white envelope and slid it over to Cooper. She slid it behind the basket of popcorn shrimp and Cooper's fish tacos so none of the other patrons could see. Cooper took it and didn't even bother looking inside. He trusted Stephanie and knew she would have done as he had asked.

"Thanks," he said, stuffing the envelope into his back pocket. He felt the thickness of the cash inside and it made him a little uneasy.

"The bank account only has about five thousand dollars in it," Stephanie said. "Well, now that I withdrew that five hundred for you, it's less than that. How are you going to get by without a real job?"

"I have some extra cash," Cooper said. "Royalty money from the book. I also took advantage of people thinking I was dead and had my friend help me sell some stuff online. My old journals, equipment, stuff like that."

"That's fiendish of you," she said, but couldn't suppress her smile. "How much?"

"About twenty-five grand."

"It might sound like a lot, but it'll be gone before you know it."

Cooper grinned and rested his hand on the book that still sat on the table between them. "Well, if things get tight, I always have this to fall back on."

"Writing? About your usual stuff?"

"Maybe."

"I don't see you ever using a pen name," she said. "You're too full of yourself."

He grinned, but the comment stung. The Cooper she had known *had* been entirely too full of himself. He really wanted to let her in on the kind of man he was now—about how he had changed. He wanted to tell her everything that had happened to him since he had returned from—well, from some place that still remained a mystery to him.

But now was not the time. She had agreed to help him with a certain set of tasks that he knew might end up blowing up in his face. When he knew for certain that what he had planned was going to either succeed or fail, then he'd tell her.

Or so he told himself.

"Things are different now," was all he said.

"Am I allowed to ask how?"

He shrugged and sipped from his beer. "I want to help other people," he said. "All of the things I know, I want to try to put it to good use." He nodded toward the book as he said this.

"Helping others while still *grasping the fringes*, huh?"

"Something like that."

"And the first people you want to help are here in Kill Devil Hills?"

"Yeah. You said you got the address, right?"

"Yes. Jenny and Sam Blackstock. It's in the envelope. You mean to tell me that you haven't even called them?"

"No, I haven't."

"So you're just going to drop by?" she asked. "You're just going to tell these people that you found a newspaper article about them and you think you can help. Is that about right?"

"That's it, exactly."

"Going in confident with guns blazing," Stephanie said. "Some things *don't* change, it seems."

"Guilty. Hey, how long are you staying here at the beach?"

"Two days. Then it's back to work."

"You want to grab dinner tonight?"

She eyed him skeptically. He could feel it even from behind the Aviators. "Let me think about it."

"Where are you staying?"

"Wouldn't you like to know?" she said. "Now shut up and eat your lunch."

He laughed and had to look away from her. It hurt him to realize that he may have missed his opportunity with Stephanie Pagent. It made him wonder what other opportunities he had missed while chasing a ridiculous career and trying to be larger than life. What had he missed during the three months he'd gone missing and the five months he'd spent in solitude since he had returned?

He took another gulp of his beer and looked out to the ocean. He watched the waves rolling in and then glanced to Stephanie. She was looking at him like she used to, with a cute sort of curiosity but an underlying skepticism.

It felt nice.

It felt familiar.

And for now, that was all Cooper could ask for.

THREE

With two beers and a large order of fish tacos in his stomach, Cooper pulled his car into the small dirt driveway in front of the Blackstock residence. There was another car in the driveway, a good sign that there might be someone home. This is where Stephanie's address had led him and, the moment he saw it, he knew it was the right place.

The residence was a cozy beach house located about a quarter of a mile away from the last of the year-round rentals outside of Kill Devil Hills. The driveway was bordered with decorative driftwood and the scraggly beach weeds that seemed to grow on most every small dune on the east coast. Little flecks of shattered seashells were strewn all around the border.

He parked the car and stepped out, trying to imagine what it must be like to arrive home every day and see a limitless expanse of ocean from your driveway. He felt inside his pocket, making sure he had the articles he had printed out. He doubted he'd need it, but it made him feel prepared for the awkward encounter that was just moments away.

He walked to the front door, taking in the exquisitely maintained house. In comparison to the rentals he had passed on the way here, it was radiant. Even the small wooden porch was finely polished and clean.

He knocked on the front door, which was adorned by a small wooden sign in the shape of a sand dollar. The word BLACK-STOCK was craved into it.

Cooper was admiring this when a woman answered the door. She looked sleepy and as if she was in a hurry. She gave Cooper an inquisitive stare and inched back behind the partially opened door.

"Hello?" Jenny Blackstock said. "Can I help you?"

"I'm not sure," Cooper answered, realizing that he wasn't quite sure how to approach the topic he needed to breach. Maybe he should have planned ahead a bit better.

"Okay…" Jenny said.

"I'm actually here because I think I might be able to help you."

Wow, that sounded cheesy, Cooper thought as he watched the woman inch back even further. He figured he probably had about five seconds and one more comment before she closed the door in his face. And maybe only ten before she called the police.

"I'm sorry," Cooper said. "That was a terribly stupid thing for me to say. Let me try again. Is that okay?"

The woman said nothing. She only nodded slowly, not really appearing afraid, but awkwardly curious. Cooper knew that there was nothing immediately threatening about his appearance. At just under six feet tall and with cheeks that always appeared slightly pudgy despite his well-maintained frame, most people tended to assume that he was friendly by nature.

"Are you Jenny Blackstock?"

"Yes. And you are…?"

"My name is Cooper Reid. I was hoping I could talk to you about the weird events you've been experiencing in your home."

Her curiosity shifted into shock. She pushed the door closed a bit more but still did not shut it completely. She remained quiet, and Cooper used her hesitation to his advantage. He reached into his pocket and took out the two articles he had printed out in a public library five days ago. He unfolded the first one and held it out to her with caution.

"This is you, right?" he said.

She looked to the article and her cheeks flushed with red. She looked up from the article, titled **A Haunted Beachfront Home**, and into Cooper's face.

"Where did you get this?" she asked.

"The internet. The site isn't very well known. But the guys that write for it do great research and are very reliable."

Jenny was clearly mad now and was having no more of it. She shook her head and looked to the floor. "Please leave," she said as politely as she could while closing the door. It fell softly into its frame, leaving Cooper to look at the little decorative sand dollar again.

Defeated, Cooper looked back down to the article. He folded it up slowly and then placed it back into his pocket. He had been expecting his initial conversation with the Blackstocks to be awkward, but not a straight-out failure. He hadn't expected this at all.

He still held the other folded article in his hands, not wanting the two articles to be connected, but somehow certain they were. And now the one solid lead he had on both of them was refusing to speak to him.

This made no sense. He had *known* to come here. In many ways, he had been *asked* to come here—although the Blackstocks clearly knew nothing about that. And honestly, Cooper wasn't sure he had a full grasp on it, either.

Not sure of what else to do, Cooper leaned forward and rested his hand on the front door, just below the little sand dollar ornament. He closed his eyes and focused on the texture of the wooden door beneath his palm. He tried to get a better sense of the place without the aid of sight, guided by only the feel of the door beneath his hand.

The porch smelled of sunlit wood but was almost entirely overpowered by the smell of the ocean behind the house—the pungent but not unpleasant aroma of strong salt. He took all of this in and listened to the muted roar of the sea, the crying of gulls nearby and, somewhere a few blocks over, someone cranking a motorcycle to life. His focus kept going back to the ocean and the slow yet hectic rhythm of the waves as they crashed along the shore.

Hearing that, Cooper got what he needed.

He pictured the waves at dusk, colored an aquatic golden green that no painter could ever get quite right. He saw this and he heard screaming in his head.

He saw the image of a young boy standing along the edge of the sea, looking out and pointing. The boy was wearing a pair of swimming trunks with a cartoon shark grinning widely and giving a thumbs-up.

The boy was saying something as he pointed out to the ocean, but Cooper wasn't sure what it was. He had tousled black hair and a slight scratch along his right temple.

Cooper saw all of this with eerie definition, as if the boy were standing directly beside him on the front porch.

Then, in a flash, the boy was gone. More screaming followed as the vision, or whatever it was, began to dissipate. The new screams were the terror-choked wails of a woman, and—

Cooper opened his eyes and looked to the Blackstocks' front door. He touched the sand dollar ornament gingerly. His heart was hammering and he could still hear the ghost sounds of the beach—not the same waves he was hearing right now from behind the house, but the crashing waves of some other time, some other afternoon long ago.

With his stomach in knots, Cooper raised his hand and knocked on the door again.

Twenty seconds passed without an answer. Cooper knocked louder, this time leaning against the door.

"Mrs. Blackstock," he called loudly, not in a shout but loud enough to be heard through the door. "I think I really need to speak with you. I think I can help you with your problems. And I think I can help you learn about what happened to Henry."

Henry, he thought. *Where the hell did that come from?*

He knocked once more and as he was rapping against the wood, the door opened. Jenny Blackstock stared at him with fury in her eyes.

"What does that article say about my son?" she asked. "What does it say about Henry?"

Cooper retrieved the article from his pocket again and handed it to her.

"Nothing," Cooper said. "That's something I picked up on my own."

"Where? How?"

Cooper winced at the question and did his best to give her a smile. Instead, it felt like his face was crooked. "I can explain it as best as I can if you'll give me just five minutes of your time."

Jenny considered this for a moment, slowly folding the article back up. "You know about Henry?"

"I think so."

She said nothing and Cooper used the moment to hand her the second article, unfolding it for her.

"Have you heard about this?" he asked.

She took the paper slowly, clearly still not trusting the stranger at her doorstep.

The headline read: LOCAL 11 YEAR OLD BOY DROWNS.

The first few sentences summed it all up: eleven year old Kevin Owens had drowned two months ago. It had been quick— so quick that his parents weren't entirely sure what had happened.

And it had happened eerily close to the Blackstock residence.

"Sounds eerily familiar, doesn't it?" Cooper asked.

Jenny nodded as a tear spilled from her left eye. She looked to Cooper as if he had just smacked her across the face.

Still, she stepped aside and let him through the door.

"Five minutes," she said. "But you don't start until my husband gets home."

FOUR

FOUR

Cooper sat in the Blackstocks's well-decorated living room, sipping from a soda that Jenny had given him without having to ask for it. She had called her husband at work and informed Cooper that he would be arriving in about twenty minutes. That twenty minutes was spent with Cooper sitting in a recliner in the living room while Jenny stood at the bar in the kitchen. She was reading and re-reading the articles Cooper had given her. She cast him the occasional glance, looking at him like a jogger might eye a suspicious-looking stray dog on the other side of the street.

"Do you know the people that wrote this article?" Jenny asked. "The one about my son, I mean."

"No, not personally."

"How do they get their information?"

"Lots of ways. Anyone you've spoken to about what's going on in your house can be a source. Cops, ghost hunting teams, church members, stuff like that."

"Church members?"

"Yes. A lot of times, people with a strong faith in God will get members of their church involved when dealing with para-normal issues. Some just for the prayer, but others in the hopes that a spiritual or demonic force might be cast out. In *your* case, though, based on the site I got the article from, I can almost guarantee that they got the information from a paranormal investigation team. Have you guys had anyone like that in your house since this all started happening?"

"Yes," Jenny said in a tone that indicated it was a decision she regretted. "About four months ago."

"Did they find anything?"

"No. They tried to blame most of it on how the wind comes through the eaves on the back porch."

"Do you mind if I have a look?"

"Not until Sam gets home," she answered, her words sharp and precise.

Cooper nodded. He wasn't about to push the issue. He understood that she wanted her husband home, not only so they could both hear what he had to say, but just in case the strange man she had never met and invited into their home turned out to be insane and tried to hurt her. He had no doubt that was why she was standing at the kitchen bar while he sat down. She was standing roughly two feet from the large wooden block that held all of the knives, perched along the end of the bar. Also, standing on her feet gave her ample opportunity to get a head start if he came after her.

Of course, he intended to do nothing of the sort. But he understood her line of reason.

When they heard the front door open and close beneath them, Jenny dashed across the room and out of Cooper's sight. She didn't say a word or even glance at him. But seconds later, he could hear Jenny and Sam Blackstock whispering softly to one another from elsewhere in the house.

It was a peculiar feeling; it made him feel like he was a child in school that had been sent to the principal's office. The whispered voices behind him could have easily been a teacher and the principal trying to determine his punishment.

A few seconds later, Sam and Jenny came into the living room as a unified force. They were holding hands when they sat down on the couch across from Cooper. Sam Blackstock was a man of average size but the fire in is gaze made him look momentarily fierce. He wasted no time, leaning forward and looking directly into Cooper's eyes. The man looked furious and a little hurt. His dark eyes were eerily similar to the eyes Cooper had seen on Henry in his vision—*vision*, or whatever it had been.

When Sam spoke, that anger came out in each word.

"The fact that I have no idea who you are and that you came here today talking about my son does two things to me," Sam said. "First, it makes me angrier than you can imagine. And second, it creeps me out. So we're going to give you your five minutes. And if you say anything to upset my wife or anger me, you and I are going to have problems. Am I understood?"

"Yes," Cooper said.

Though Sam Blackstock was about the same size and build as Cooper, there would not be much of a fight. Of course, Sam didn't know that Cooper had several years of FBI training under his belt.

Sometimes, even Cooper forgot. He had never been the most physical of specimens, but he was more than capable of handling himself in a fight. During his time with the bureau, he'd taken down men much larger than Sam Blackstock. Still, he was not about to underestimate the strength and determination of a man that had lost a child.

Cooper began the only way he knew how. As he started, he hoped those old writer instincts would kick in and he'd be able to get the right words out.

"My name is Cooper Reid," he started. "Once upon a time, I was pretty well-known for some work that, looking back on it, was pretty ridiculous. Before all of that, though, I worked as a field agent for the FBI for a few years. I was recruited out of the FBI and into another organization that was overseen mostly by the CIA with some support from the Department of Homeland Security."

"Do you have ID?" Sam asked.

Cooper shook his head nervously. "I don't. I'm quite fortunate to not work for the government anymore. But if you have any doubts, a simple Google search will show you that I'm telling the truth. I got into some hot water with just about every government organization I was involved with because of a book I wrote. It was a blip on the news a few years back."

It was clear that the Blackstocks knew nothing about the Cooper M. Reid controversy that had hummed beneath the headlines three years ago. But neither of them made a move for the laptop that was sitting on a small desk on the far side of the living room to check on his story.

Cooper took the opportunity to continue. He did so with caution, knowing that this would be the tricky area.

"My line of expertise was in the paranormal. Only, the FBI, CIA, and Homeland Security never called it that. At one time, I had a good reputation with the FBI. It was so good that I was approached by a ghost organization that I don't think even exists anymore. They were sort of headhunting because of my interests and my fields of study. I have a degree in astrobiology and was an expert in the field of parapsychology."

"Parapsychology?" Jenny asked, incredulous. So far, it looked like she was absolutely not buying the story. "Are you kidding me?"

"No."

"You mean like mind-reading and making things float with your mind?" Sam asked.

Cooper nodded. "The organization that hired me was deep into that sort of thing. They sent me around the world to investigate some very strange cases. Some were crime-based in nature but many were simple occurrences of the paranormal: haunted houses, UFOs, demonic possession and things of that nature."

"I thought those sorts of government programs were just urban legends and crazy rumors," Sam said, his doubt thick and pronounced in his voice. "You're talking about things like MK Ultra and Project Blue Book, right?"

Cooper shrugged. "That's just the tip of the iceberg, really. And it's also straying from my point."

"Which is?" Jenny asked.

"I lost my job because of the book I wrote," Cooper explained. "The government tried to keep me quiet, but I started researching cases on my own. I did that for a little over a year, collecting information for another book. But then I happened upon one particular case and something happened to me. To be honest, I'm still not sure *what* happened. But according to everything I've read and things I've been told, I went missing for a little over three months."

"Our son..." Jenny said, anger causing her voice to tremble. "You really think we'd let you talk about the death of our son and the craziness going on in our house in some book?"

"No. Not at all. There's no book. I'm done with that. See, when I came back from—from wherever I was—I started getting these sorts of visions. I'd get gut reactions to things I saw or read. I tried ignoring them but it wouldn't stop. Finally, I decided I had to see what was going on. And if I'm being honest, I'm more interested in finding out what these visions and gut feelings are than what is happening in your house. I'm just putting that out there for the sake of transparency."

"I don't believe any of this," Sam said, getting to his feet. "I'm going to ask you to leave now, Mr. Reid. And if you do it now without argument, I won't call the police."

"I understand," Cooper said, also standing. "But the clock in your kitchen tells me that I have one of my five minutes remaining. I just have one more thing I need to tell you."

Sam stepped forward and Cooper saw his clenched fists right away. But Jenny reached out and took her husband's wrist. He looked back to her, angry and hesitant, but there was a shaky sort of understanding that passed between them.

"Thirty seconds," Jenny said in a near-hiss.

"I saw your story on that site I was telling you about—the one about your haunted beach house. And then when I did some research on the area, I also found the recent story of Kevin Owens and how he drowned. There was a definite connection, but I thought it seemed too small. Simple, almost. So I came out here, not knowing why. Up until today, I didn't even know your son's name or that he had died. All I knew was that you had reported laughing children in your home at night. I knew *nothing* about your son until I was standing out on your porch. After Jenny closed the door on me the first time, I put my hand on the door and…and I just *knew*."

"Get out," Jenny said. She was crying, slowly sinking into the couch.

Sam was staring Cooper down, not budging. His face was a stark sheet of rage.

Cooper wrapped up, fully expecting a blow from Sam. If it came, Cooper decided that he wouldn't even block it. He'd let the man have his release. He couldn't begin to imagine what this must feel like for them.

But Cooper went on. He had to. He was certain of it in a way that he did not fully understand.

"It was late in the afternoon," Cooper said quietly, looking to the floor. "He was wearing swim trunks with a smiling shark giving a thumbs-up. He was pointing at something out at sea. Something close to land, I think. He was shouting something…I don't know what. He was—"

He wasn't interrupted by a punch from Sam Blackstock like he'd been expecting. Instead, Sam let out a stifled cry and slowly sank into the couch beside his wife. They both looked up to Cooper as if he had done some great magic trick. There was sick wonder in their faces but there was fear, too.

"How could you know that?" Jenny asked in a whisper.

"I don't know. It literally just came to me on your front porch."

"No one could know all of that," Sam said. "We were the

only ones on the beach. We were the only ones that saw it. The pointing and what he said…we never said anything about it."

"We didn't even tell the coroner or police…we didn't tell anyone what he had been shouting," Jenny said. "It was too strange—sort of scary. We didn't want to dwell on the fact that those words were the last thing he ever said."

"Can I ask—" Cooper began.

"Dark water," Jenny said, wiping a tear away. "That's the last thing our baby ever said. *Dark water.*"

FIVE

Cooper didn't think the shock had worn off yet, nor did he think the Blackstocks fully believed him. Regardless, they no longer asked him to leave and, in fact, invited him to stay and check out their house. They started at the front porch, something Cooper secretly hadn't wanted to do. He feared that if he saw that image again—the sight of a boy that he now knew had been Henry Blackstock—he might bail on this entire trip.

But his return visit to the porch turned up nothing of the sort. He looked at the sand dollar ornament on the door as if it might bite him, but the vision never came back. He *did* sense it though. He felt that, if he wanted, he could close his eyes and focus, and he'd be able to pluck the vision right out of the air as if it were a passing insect.

The Blackstocks led him back inside, showing him every room in the house. Sam led them through while Jenny did most of the talking. The house was built like most every other beach house in the area. Downstairs consisted of a small foyer that instantly led to more stairs. To the right, there was a modest-sized office and another door that led out onto a small patio. Sam led them through the office and into a smaller room that sat off the back of the office.

"This was supposed to be a guest bedroom," Jenny said. "But we really don't get much company. My mom stayed a few times after Henry died, but that's about it. On one of the nights we heard the laughing—one of the very first times, I think that was —we were pretty sure it came from here."

She stepped aside as Cooper checked out the room. A twin bed rested in the corner and a small table sat next to it, decorated with a lamp and a large conk shell.

"Nothing was out of place when you checked it out following the laughter?" he asked.

"Not a thing."

Sam led them upstairs, back into the living room. As Cooper looked around, it occurred to him that he had, less than ten minutes ago, vaguely told the Blackstocks about his peculiar disappearance. While he had told only one other person about it since his return, he had not spoken about it at such length with anyone. The Blackstocks had been the first. In a way, it felt good to get it off of his chest, but he also felt vulnerable and exposed.

"Down the hall," Jenny said, "there's just the bathroom, the master bedroom and Henry's room. We haven't changed a thing since the day he died."

Cooper's old investigative instincts wanted to ask if he could have a look. But he knew that he had already dealt these grieving parents a huge load this afternoon. He wouldn't dare tread on such sacred ground without first being invited. Besides, he didn't think that was where he needed to go. Snooping around their dead son's room wasn't why he had come to Kill Devil Hills.

"And nothing out of the ordinary has ever happened in any of those rooms?" Cooper asked.

"No. It's always just...*laughing*," Sam said.

"Sometimes it sounds like it's coming from outside," Jenny added. "But usually it's in the living room. Once on the stairs, once downstairs, but from the living room most of the time."

"And then there's the last time we heard it," Sam said. "It

was moving around. Sort of playing with us. It knocked a bowl off of the bar over there and then there were—"

"Footsteps," Cooper said, the word simply springing from his mouth. He glanced around the room, his eyes narrowed. "But not in *here*. Not in the living room. They were...."

He was barely aware that Sam and Jenny Blackstock both looked terrified. He understood that he had just revealed something that had not been in the article. Again, it was another detail that only they knew.

Cooper had no idea where it had come from. It simply appeared in his head like a bold ghost, demanding to be discovered. It came to him like a memory that had been there all along, hiding in the ether of his mind.

"There?" Cooper asked, pointing into the dining area.

Jenny nodded. "Yeah."

Cooper walked into the dining room and, not sure why, knelt down to the carpet. He ran his hand along it and, after a few seconds, shook his head.

"I'm not getting much else. What can you tell me about the footsteps?"

"They were small," Sam said, his voice distant. He was looking at Cooper like a man that was rediscovering his childhood fear of the dark. "Sort of soft and light, you know?"

"They were bare, too," Jenny said. "You could clearly see the toes on a few of them. They were unmistakably a child's footprints. The prints were wet, like a child had just gotten out of the tub."

"Or the ocean," Sam said.

At the mention of the ocean, Cooper looked up to the sliding glass door. The blinds were open, giving him a stellar view of the beach. He watched a wave crest, break, and then crash gently onto the sand. From where he knelt in the Blackstocks's dining room, it sounded like soft static.

"Forgive me for asking," Cooper said. "But do you think it was Henry?"

"No," Jenny said. "The laughter we heard that night was of a little girl."

Cooper got back to his feet, again looking back out to the beach. He walked to the sliding glass door and observed their back porch.

"The prints led out here, right?"

"Yes," Jenny said. "I saw them on the back porch, leading towards the beach."

"Do you mind if I go out and look around?"

It was the first time he had asked their permission for anything and he knew just how pivotal a moment it was. He was relieved when they both nodded their heads. Sam stepped forward and slid the door open for him.

Cooper stepped out onto the back porch and looked around. A patio table and two chairs sat to the far right side. A very expensive-looking grill sat to the left. Other than that, there really wasn't much to see. The porch itself was very nicely made, just like the rest of the house.

It then occurred to him that while the Blackstocks might not necessarily be wealthy, they certainly lived comfortably; the beachfront house said as much. In Cooper's experience, the cases of fraudulent paranormal claims came from people seeking attention, hoping that some reporter or television network would come to their doorstep with a check. But the Blackstocks did not appear to be those sorts of people.

Besides…there was the terribly accurate vision he'd had on the front porch and seeing a series of footprints on the carpet for just a split second that needed to be considered. Those things had been *more* than enough to convince Cooper that the Black-stocks were legitimately experiencing something.

Cooper looked out toward the back of the Blackstocks's prop-erty and the beach beyond. The back porch stairs led down onto a small and scraggly stretch of lawn. A few decorative flat stones ran along the center of the grass, ending at the same crafty combination of driftwood and tall grass that he had seen out front. Directly after these, the beach began. Cooper looked out to the ocean and thought he could understand how people could fall so in love with living here.

"Did you see any sort of disturbance in the yard?" Cooper asked.

"No," Jenny said. "From what I could tell, the prints stopped at the porch. It was dark, though. The porch lights don't really reach far beyond the stairs."

Cooper walked down the steps, not sure what he was looking for. If he was being honest with himself (something he was usually not very good about doing), he was waiting for one of those flashes or visions or whatever they were, to hit him. But so far, he was getting nothing.

"I have some more questions," he said. "But if I cross any sort of line, just let me know."

Sam let out a nervous laugh. "You somehow knew things that no one but Jenny and I knew. If there's a line to be crossed, I think it's already been obliterated. Just ask."

Cooper nodded towards the beach that lay on the other side of their yard. "Was that the stretch of beach where your son died?"

"No," Jenny said. "It was about a quarter mile down that way."

When she pointed to the left, Cooper thought he saw her hand trembling.

"We go there sometimes," Sam said. "To remember him, you know? It hurts like hell, but it also seems sort of fitting."

"Seems crazy right?" Jenny asked.

"I wouldn't know," Cooper answered.

Secretly, though, he was wondering why the parents of a boy that had drowned so close to the beach would elect to remain in a house that was only a quarter of a mile away from where he drowned. Sentimentality, perhaps.

Cooper had never had kids and, if his life continued on the course it was currently on, he likely never would. He didn't want to assume anything about parents that had lost a child. He already felt like a monumental jerk for making them go digging into the memories of their son's death.

"Did either of you know about Kevin Owens?" Cooper asked.

"We heard about it on the news," Sam said. "I saw the headline in the paper but skipped it. I can't read about things like that without automatically picturing Henry."

"Do you know *where* Kevin Owens drowned?" Cooper asked, although he already knew. He simply didn't want to be the one to deliver the news.

When Jenny nodded, he let out a sigh of relief.

"Pretty close to where Henry drowned," she said. The expression on her face said it all. She had also made the connection and it had rattled her.

Cooper let a moment of silence hang among them before he asked the next question.

"Would it be okay if I walked down there?" he asked. "To where Henry died?"

Neither of the Blackstocks said anything. Cooper kept his gaze out to sea, letting them have their silence without feeling pressured. He could feel the tension coming off of them. It felt like he was at the funeral of someone he barely knew, feeling the eyes of most of those in attendance staring at him as they tried to figure out who he was and why he was there.

"Come on," Sam said, walking directly past him and out into the yard. He didn't so much as glance in Cooper's direction while he walked along the flat stones towards the beach.

Jenny also avoided eye contact with Cooper as she walked down the stairs and into the yard. She followed after Sam, giving Cooper a cursory little wave to follow.

Cooper followed them across the yard and through a break in the decorative driftwood. He stepped onto the beach for the second time that day and, this time, it did not feel comforting and warm at all.

SIX

He had been following Sam and Jenny along the beach for less than thirty seconds when Cooper realized he was going to have to take his shoes off to keep up. The sand was softer here than it had been four miles down the beach where he had first glanced out at the sea earlier in the day. Both Sam and Jenny were already barefoot, as they had been in their home. He wondered if that was just something that eventually came natural to you if you lived at the beach long enough.

They walked almost directly in the center of the beach. The sea lapped at the land about twenty feet below them and the small but gradually rising dunes climbed slowly upwards in the direction of the houses to the other side. Cooper looked up towards the tiny hills, seeing the weeds that managed to look both cozy and beautiful in the sand. A small fragment of dried fence lay partially collapsed in the sand and weeds. The entire scene looked like it belonged in one of any millions of seaside paintings adorning doctor's offices and starving artist's sales.

Cooper also noticed that there were only five other homes along this stretch of land beyond the Blackstock house. After the fifth and final house, the land above the beach grew rocky and uneven. A few stubborn dunes peeked out of the rock here and there, but the majority of the land was sand, rock, and thick vegetation. Cooper couldn't see the highway through the vegetation but could catch glimpses of the tops of vehicles as they passed.

"Is that why the houses out this way aren't typically big rental attractions?" Cooper asked, pointing to the overgrown land.

"Mostly," Jenny said. "We've had a few friends suggest that we rent the house out for the summer, though. Out here, where it's quiet and the business of the main stretch comes to an end, there really isn't much demand. But elderly couples and big families apparently prefer these sorts of areas."

"How much further does it go on like this?"

"About two miles," Sam said. "All of this comes to an end almost out of nowhere. There's quiet beach and some pretty stunning scenery. But then all of a sudden, there's a pier for fishing and a bunch of tee shirt shops."

"And on the day your son died, were you just out for a walk?" Cooper asked.

"Yeah," Jenny said. "Up ahead, you can just barely see where there are some pretty big rocks sticking up out of the ocean. See them?"

Cooper looked ahead and saw what she was referencing. There were two rather large black rock outcroppings sticking out of the sea; one of them stood about ten feet above the water. They looked to be roughly the same color and texture of the rocky terrain to his left.

"Yes, I see them."

"Well, there are a few sandbars out there, too," Jenny went on. "You can go out to where the water comes up to your waist and then, all of a sudden, you start walking back *up*. You can go about twenty feet out on a few of those sandbars and the water never gets any higher than your knees. We used to take Henry out there. He loved it. He really liked it during the evening when the sun was going down. It's quite beautiful."

Cooper noticed that as she said this, she reached out and took Sam's hand. Sam gave his wife's hand a squeeze and they shared a smile. In that moment, Cooper decided that he liked Sam and Jenny Blackstock a great deal. And he felt worse than ever for having dragged up these painful memories for them.

After another three minutes or so, Sam and Jenny suddenly came to a stop. They were still hand in hand, looking out to the ocean together. They were roughly a hundred yards or so away from the large black rocks that Jenny had pointed out moments ago.

"This is where it happened," Jenny said. "And to this day, I'm still not sure *how* it happened. It happened so fast…"

"I'm sorry to put you through this," Cooper said. "Really, I am. I honestly don't even know why I came. I don't know why—"

"It's okay," Sam said. "I don't know what your deal is—if you're some kind of psychic or something—but if you know the things you know and claim to know what happened to Henry, we can wrestle with all of this one more time."

"I'm not a psychic. I'm not sure what to call this, actually."

That much was true. Ever since he had reappeared, he'd been getting those hunches and brief little visions from time to time. He was no psychic, that was for sure. Whatever this thing was that had been itching at him was far beyond the reaches of any psychics he had ever met…and he had met quite a few in his time.

"Sam and I were sitting right here," Jenny said, making a little dent in the sand with her toe. "Henry was right there, standing in the surf. The water was no higher than his knees. And he knew that the sandbars don't reach out here, so he was staying close to the shore. He was bending over and sort of sifting through the sand for seashells. He especially liked the ones that were peach-colored."

"Not orange, though" Sam said, smiling. "No. Peach."

Jenny and Sam laughed softly at this. Cooper assumed it was

some sort of inside joke between the members of their family. It made him feel like an intruder.

"Sam and I were talking," Jenny continued. "I even remember that we were talking about finally letting Henry take surfing lessons. We knew Henry was old enough and would put the time and energy into it. He was nine and all he had talked about that summer was surfing. We were trying to figure out which one of the instructors would maybe be best for him and that's when he started shouting."

"It wasn't a scared shout," Sam said. "It was just sort of a shout of surprise. You know? He was pointing out there, towards those rocks."

Sam pointed to the two large black rocks that stuck up from the ocean, a little less than twenty yards out from where the waves were currently lapping at the shore. He pointed, but he did not look at them.

"Dark water," Sam said. "That's all Henry said. We both looked in that direction to see what he was talking about but there was nothing. Just the rocks."

Jenny picked it up from there. She wasn't crying but Cooper could tell that she was having to make an effort to keep it together.

"We didn't take our eyes away from him for any more than three seconds," she said. "It *couldn't* have been any more than that. But when we looked back to him, he was already under the water. It was like some wave came up out of nowhere and pulled him under. He was a long way out from where he had been before we looked away to those rocks. If it was an undertow, it was faster and stronger that any I've ever felt or even heard of."

"I ran out there after him," Sam said. "I saw him when I got to the water and still saw him when the first wave hit me. They were small waves—nothing big but just strong enough to knock you back a little, you know? But after a few seconds, I couldn't see him anymore. Not even a hand coming out of the water. Nothing. He was just gone."

He fell silent here. Even the waves seemed to go quiet out of respect.

"I swam out there, going under and dragging at the bottom with my hands," Sam continued. "I never found him. Nothing. I was out there until I just about passed out. Jenny told me later that I was swimming out there looking for Henry for almost half an hour. She called the life guard station in that time. They had to drag me out."

"And the lifeguards weren't able to find his body?" Cooper asked.

"No," Jenny said. "No one ever did. Not the police, not the search and rescue units, not the volunteers that pooled together right after it happened."

"Is that common?"

"It happens every now and then. Sometimes bodies that go under near a beach get pulled out to sea. It depends on how far away from the shore they are. But Henry was pretty close. After the service we had for him, the search and rescue guys basically gave up and said there might always be that call weeks or months later once his body washed up on a shore somewhere. But that never happened."

Cooper felt his heart sinking. He couldn't remember a time in his life where he had ever felt such compassion for someone. He felt deflated and sad. It was something that the Cooper M. Reid prior to his disappearance would have never been capable of.

"I'm truly sorry," Cooper said.

"Don't be," Jenny said. "Just…I don't know. I sound like an idiot for even suggesting it, but if you think there's something you might be able to find out with whatever it is you have…then I think we're willing to be available."

She looked to Sam, as if for confirmation, and he nodded his agreement. "Yeah," he said. "Anything about Henry *or* what might be happening in our house. I don't like the idea of what-ever it is you're able to do but…"

"But after all this time, I think we deserve some answers," Jenny finished for him.

Cooper looked out to those two black rocks, breaking out of the sea. He had noticed right away that the Blackstocks had not taken him directly to them. He also noticed how Jenny and Sam would not look at the tall rocks for very long, not even when speaking directly about them.

He could see nothing particularly sinister about the rock formations and wasn't getting any sort of gut reaction when he looked at them. But if they were the last thing Henry Blackstock had shown an interest in before he died, Cooper supposed they would be the best place to start looking for answers.

Of course, it went a bit deeper than that, and he almost didn't want to voice it.

But he knew he had to. And even before he started speaking, he felt the familiar chill of a case starting to come together. He handed Sam the article on the drowning of Kevin Owens, the paper now feeling almost as if it had some sort of supernatural weight to it.

"Kevin Owens died over there," Cooper said, pointing to the beach beyond the black rocks. "As you can see in the article, it's a story very similar to yours."

Sam read it over, blinking away tears. He handed it to Jenny but she shook her head, wanting nothing to do with it. She'd already read it once while she and Cooper had been waiting on Sam. Cooper assumed that had been more than enough.

"Have you talked to the Owens family?" Jenny asked.

"No," Cooper said. "From what I can gather, they left town. I'll be honest…I was able to get your address by less-than-honest means. I tried the same with the Owens family and all I found out was that they left for the summer. They left Kill Devil Hills five days after their son died. I'm not sure where they went."

For that, he considered himself fortunate. From just hearing the story of Henry Blackstock's death, Cooper was basically drained. He'd had a few pretty surreal moments since his return

five months ago and the last two hours were quickly beginning
to top the list.

He wasn't sure he'd be able to go through this again with
another family.

Sam seemed to pick up on his mood right away. He clapped
Cooper on the back with hesitancy to his touch. Cooper understood it; although they had just shared something pretty significant, they still found his abilities a bit scary. It was an unspoken
understanding that he could feel coming off them like heat.

"Come on," Sam said. "Let's head back to the house and grab
a beer."

Cooper nodded and let Sam and Jenny lead him back to their
house.

When he finally turned away from the tall black rocks
peeking out of the water, Cooper almost felt as if they were
watching them leave.

SEVEN

S am insisted that he stay for a few more beers, but Cooper had politely declined. He knew that, if he stayed around, the Blackstocks would start asking him more about his history and how he had come by his peculiar set of skills. And since that skillset now apparently consisted of having dream-like visions of real people and real events that he had no control over, it wasn't a conversation he was ready to have just yet. So he allowed himself a single beer with both of them on their back porch, watching the sea as it tugged in the dusk. Sharing a drink with them seemed like the least he could do after dragging them back through the painful memories of the death of their son.

He left with only the vaguest mention of possibly coming back to see them. They had not seemed overwhelmed when he'd taken his leave but Cooper still had the idea that there would be a few tears shed in their house before they went to sleep. And quite a bit of conversation about the freak that had showed up on their doorstep. Leaving the Blackstocks to the unanswered questions about Henry's death, Cooper headed for his hotel, tired and wiped out.

The hotel he was staying at was a modest little dive that boasted mediocre rooms. None of the rooms offered any sort of view of the beach, although the ocean was in plain sight from the parking lot. The occasional determined weed poked up from the blacktop and the hotel exterior looked like it had been made with stucco, glue, and nothing else. But it was cheap and it had a bed; those were the only features that Cooper cared about.

When he arrived at his room, Cooper thought he might have a pizza delivered and crash in front of the television until he fell asleep. It wasn't exactly how he had envisioned his first trip out into the world to test his new abilities, but it's what he wanted in that moment. The experience with the Blackstocks had exhausted him more than he'd expected. He was sure he'd end up waking up around two or three in the morning—something that seemed to happen more and more these days—and he might take the next step in figuring out what was going on in the Blackstocks's house.

But for now, he wanted to rest.

As he collapsed on the bed, he saw that the red message light was flashing on the phone on the bedside table. He dialed the desk operator and asked for his message. He was surprised to find that Stephanie had called him. He had missed her call by less than half an hour. He jotted down the number as the clerk recited it to him and hung up before the man on the other end could finish asking if there was anything else Cooper needed.

Cooper punched the number into the relic of a phone—the kind with square buttons and a cord connecting the receiver to the cradle. Stephanie answered on the second ring and Cooper was slightly annoyed by how much the sound of her voice could still lift his spirits.

"That took longer than I thought it would," she said, skipping formalities like *hello*. "Things went well with the Blackstocks, I take it?"

"I guess. Things went *weird*. Not particularly well."

"Did they call the police or have you committed?"

"No."

"Then I'd say things went well."

"Good point."

"You want to tell me about it?"

"I don't know. Maybe."

"Well, that's the only way I'm going to agree to have dinner with you," she said with a chuckle.

"Fine. Just tell me where to pick you up."

"Nice try. I'll be by your place in about an hour."

"I used to be an FBI agent, you know. It won't be hard to figure it out."

"Yeah, but don't."

"Okay. So hey, why did you give me the number to your hotel? Why not just give me your cell phone number so I can always have it?"

"Because you'd always have it. I don't think we're there yet."

Cooper laughed lightly at this, although he wasn't sure if it was meant to be a funny jab or not.

Again skipping formalities, Stephanie didn't bother with a *bye* or a *see ya* or anything of the sort. She simply hung up. Cooper grinned at the receiver in his hand and then placed it back in the cradle.

He looked to the bed and realized that after talking to Stephanie, he wasn't quite as tired as he had been five minutes ago.

COOPER SHOWERED but didn't bother dressing nicely. Even if he'd wanted to, the only nice clothes he had in his single suitcase was a poorly maintained black suit that he had packed just in case he needed to fake his old roots and pose as an FBI agent. He still had his old ID to go with it. He kept it tucked away at the bottom of the suitcase like a family heirloom he resented but could not part with. He wasn't sure if he would be able to cross that line—posing as an agent when he was doing everything he could to *not* draw attention to himself—but he also knew that the suit and the badge could often work like a charm when other creative solutions did not.

He didn't fuss over the way he looked because he knew Stephanie wouldn't, either. And when she knocked on his door exactly one hour after they had ended their call, he saw that he had been right.

Of course, with Stephanie, it never mattered. She always managed to look great, no matter what she wore. In fact, she was in the same outfit she'd been wearing when they shared their brief lunch earlier in the day, right down to the cheap flip flops. She was even still wearing her sunglasses, despite the fact that night was less than half an hour away from fully falling.

Cooper found it funny and slightly comforting to see that she had not changed much in the twenty months that had passed since they had last seen each other. They had dated quite seriously, once upon a time, but that had been nearly three years before his disappearance. Despite the break-up, they had come close to getting back together nearly a year before he'd gone missing. The fact that she was here with him, while he stood at the precipice of the next monumental moments of his life, seemed fitting. She'd always been there in the past. It seemed as if *that* was one thing that was going to stay the same, no matter how weird things got, as he tried his best to figure out what had happened to him.

"Ready?" she asked him simply, peeking over his shoulder and frowning at the small room.

"Yeah, let's go."

Without a word, she turned and led him to her car. The silence fit them well, sliding around them comfortably. It was not an awkward silence, but one that was filled with unspoken thoughts that the other could practically read. For Cooper, it was thoughts of how he felt that Stephanie had not changed much... thoughts about how he'd like to pick things up where they had left off roughly twenty months ago.

Stephanie's silence, on the other hand, spoke of reluctance yet, at the same time, a sort of willful obligation.

She spoke only when it was necessary as she drove them down the main strip of beach businesses. She fiddled with the radio and eventually landed on a station that was playing a Jimmy Buffet song.

"I thought you hated Buffet," Cooper said.

"I do. But we're at the beach. Might as well live it up."

"Rebel," Cooper laughed.

That was the extent of their conversation until they reached the restaurant. She chose a quaint looking place that sat on the opposite side of the beach, away from the water. When they got out of the car and walked inside, she made sure to never let him take the lead or get in front of her. He knew her well and had expected this. Stephanie had always had trust issues and didn't like to give anyone control, no matter how trivial of a situation she was in. He supposed it was why she had chosen the less than honest line of business she was in.

While she worked IT for a telecommunications firm by day, she was something of a freelance hacker by night. She made great money but lived in a small apartment where she spent most of her free time in front of a computer, talking to less-than-desirable people that shared her interest in hacking and getting their hands on sensitive information. The hacking was what paid the bills. Her 9-5 was really just a front. It had been that way since her sophomore year of college.

Cooper assessed all of this as they were led through the restaurant by a hostess. Familiar facts eased his mind. While being with Stephanie under these circumstances was awkward, to say the least, he was able to relax by reminding himself that he knew her well. He had always been in tune with her issues, quirks, and personality. No matter how stand-offish she might be, that was one fact that would never change.

And because he was so familiar with her, he was fully prepared by the onslaught of conversation that erupted from her the moment they were seated. That, too, was something familiar. Her silence had usually been the calm before a storm of interrogation-like questions. This had been true while they had been dating *and* as strictly friends.

"So, the Blackstocks," she said. "Nice people?"

Cooper laughed and shook his head. "Sorry. None of that yet. I want to know what you've been up to. I know you're still hacking, of course. Without your skills, I wouldn't be here right now. What else have you been up to?"

She took her sunglasses off and sat them at the edge of the table. She leaned forward and looked directly into his eyes.

"What is this, Cooper? And don't feed me a line of crap. You disappear from my life for about twenty months—three of which you claim to have *literally* disappeared. Then you call me to ask for my help. Would you have called me if I *couldn't* have been of help?"

"Eventually," he said.

"That's a terrible answer."

"But it's the truth."

She sighed and seemed to size him up. He looked for something like compassion in that stare but saw none.

"You can ask three questions," she said. "Make them good. After that, we're going to talk business. And since I put my ass on the line for you, *business* includes you filling me in on where you were when you disappeared. It also includes telling me what you've been doing for the last five months since you got back, and what you intend to do about the Blackstocks."

"I can answer *most* of that."

She rolled her eyes and waited for him to start. As he tried to decide on the best questions to ask, a waitress came by and took their drink orders. Stephanie ordered red wine and Cooper ordered a Coke.

"Question one," Cooper said, folding his hands and leaning into the table. He tried a smile but it felt weird. And it apparently had no effect on Stephanie. "Are you seeing anyone?"

"Not right now," she answered immediately. "After I didn't hear from you for five months, I figured you were out of the picture. So I started seeing this one guy for a while but it ended quickly."

"So you're not seeing him now?"

"Is that really what you want your second question to be?"

"No. I retract that question."

She smiled at him in a way that showed a glimpse of her rarely-seen sweet side. She knew she was in control of the conversation and didn't mind gloating about it. Still, Cooper considered the smile a small victory and asked his next question before the moment passed.

"What kind of work were you doing before I called you? And I don't mean the boring telecom stuff."

"The same old thing. I'm working with a few groups that are keeping tabs on people that are suspected of being involved in sex trafficking."

"You know, the FBI actually works on things like that....*legally.*"

"I know. They're also slow and show very few results. Do you really want to get into a debate on the effectiveness of our government? You worked for them at one time. Remember how awesome they were to you?"

"Touché. Anyway, I digress."

"Yeah...we're working on a program that infects their computer with a virus that pings a few government-owned websites. And by *ping*, I mean it leads those agencies to believe that their site is being hacked. And when they trace it, it goes back to the sex trafficker. "

"That's genius."

Stephanie smiled smugly and patted herself on the shoulder.

"What's your third question?" she asked.

Cooper had several he wanted to ask but didn't know which was the right one. "I think I'll save it for another time."

"Don't save it for too long," she said. "You have me at your disposal for tomorrow and that's about it. After that I have to get back to the cubicles of the IT world."

The waitress brought their drinks and took their orders. The moment she was gone, Stephanie started in on him. She did not allow a single moment of silence, breaking it with her usual bluntness.

"So where were you?" she asked. "Everything I could find says that you were in Kansas and then you just disappeared."

"I was."

"Where, exactly. And if you mention a tornado or Oz, I'm going to punch you in the nose."

"No, not Oz. Though that might make more sense. I honestly don't remember. It's there, in the back of my mind, but I can't pry it out just yet."

If she didn't believe him, she made no sign of it. She simply continued on. "You say you got back five months ago, but I can't find any trace of you up until you contacted me two weeks ago."

"Good," he said. "If I managed to stay under wraps well enough to elude you and your hacker networks, I must be doing pretty well. Like I said, though, I did have help."

"Yeah, who was it, by the way?"

"I have connections, too," he said slyly. "It's just a guy I knew from the bureau that got fed up with how they were doing business with wire taps and all that. When I came back from wherever I was, I asked for his help. He opened my bank accounts, got me an apartment and made sure I was untraceable —phone, internet, everything. He ended up sliding into the same line of work as you. From time to time, I think there are still some departments in the government that come to him for work."

"Interesting. But not interesting enough for me to realize that you just tried to dodge my question. Where were you, Cooper? When you disappeared, where did you go?"

"I told you. I don't remember."

"No details at all?"

"A few...maybe. But I don't know if it's even worth mentioning."

"Try me."

For the first time since sitting down at the table, Cooper looked away from her. His nerves were on edge and his heart was hammering. He'd never talked about this. The closest he had come was with the Blackstocks and even that had not really scratched the surface.

"I'm not entirely sure," he finally said.

"What does that mean?"

"It means I don't know where I was. And I have no clear recollection of the place. It was dark most of the time, I think. And it was quiet."

"Are you being purposefully vague?"

"Not at all. Steph, I want to talk to someone about what happened. I think I *need* to. But the hell of it is that I don't remember all of it. I have only the faintest memory of how I got there and absolutely *no* idea how I got out."

Stephanie began to play with her glasses, as if she was thinking of putting them back on to hide her eyes. "Are you talking about some other town?" she asked. "Or are you getting into your freaky-deaky stuff?"

"Freaky-deaky."

"Where were you, Cooper? Some other place? Some other *world?*" She didn't roll her eyes when she said it, but it was implied in her tone.

Cooper shrugged. "I really don't know. I wish I did. Seriously...I only remember a sky that looked like it was twilight all the time. Everything was plain and flat. Featureless. There are some other details that I can sort of feel at the back of my mind but they won't come."

"You understand that if you're trying to tell me that you got teleported to some other world, I'm likely not going to believe you. Right?"

"Yes, I know. Always so skeptical."

"Do you know how long you were in this place?"

"I looked back through my notes. From what I can tell, I left for Tilton, Kansas, on February twenty-first. I know I took equipment with me. I even know which equipment, but I have no idea where it is now. I would assume the FBI has it. Or at least some shadow part of the FBI."

"Maybe that branch you worked for," Stephanie suggested. "The one you would never tell me the name of."

"Probably," Cooper said, ignoring her jab. "Anyway, so let's assume I went missing on February twenty-second. When I was no longer in that other place, I found myself back in Tilton, Kansas. Seventy-two days had passed."

A look crossed Stephanie's face that was either utter disbelief or disappointment. Cooper couldn't tell which. He could almost hear the gears working in her head, trying to decide if they wanted to be in awe of this fact or if they wanted to sound the crazy-alarm.

"You mean to tell me," she said, "that you went missing for seventy-two days and you remember nothing about it?"

"That's right."

"You met no people that stick out in your mind?"

Cooper shook his head. "I don't think there were people there. I think it was just...empty. That's all I remember."

"How did you eat?"

"I don't know."

"You don't remember buildings? Landmarks? Anything?"

Cooper thought for a moment. He felt something trying to creep forward in his memories but he only caught a hazy glimpse. "I think there were mountains in the distance. Always in the distance. Like you could walk forever and never reach them. But that's it."

"Cooper...I don't even—"

The waitress came by the table with their food. Cooper decided right away that she was a good waitress. She could tell that there was a heavy conversation going on at the table and didn't bother interfering with pleasantries. She gave a simple comment of "Let me know if you need anything else," and then left them alone.

Cooper bit into his burger right away, waiting for Stephanie to pick things back up. She toyed with her flounder, poking it with her fork. She looked defeated. Cooper winced a bit internally when he realized that she also looked like she didn't want to be there.

"So," she said after a few silent moments. "Tell me about the Blackstocks."

And just like that, she let him off the hook. Either she didn't believe him and thought he was lying to her, or she believed every word of it and was terrified. Honestly, based on her history of not believing in much of anything he had ever researched, Cooper thought it was the latter.

And that was fine with him—for now.

So he told her about his afternoon with the Blackstocks, filling her in on Henry's drowning four years ago. He also told her about the odd occurrences in their house and how Jenny and Sam had taken him out to the beach, to the very spot where Henry had died.

"That's harsh," Stephanie said. "Of course, I don't believe there are ghosts in their house, but it's still a sad story."

"Still don't believe in ghosts, huh?"

"I'm not sure. I'd like to say I'm on the fence, but I sort of lean to the *no* pasture."

"How did we ever date?"

"Healthy debates, booze, and sex," she said, only half joking.

"Oh yeah. Although I don't know if I'd call the debates *healthy*."

"So what are your next steps with this family?" she asked, making sure to get the conversation away from their past relationship as fast as possible.

"I'm not entirely sure. I want to check out a few things before I bother them again. I told you about Kevin Owens, right?"

"Yes. He drowned a few months ago."

"Yeah. Two months. And he drowned about twenty feet away from the same spot Henry Blackstock drowned."

"Creepy."

"Isn't it?"

"What other things do you need to check out?"

Cooper grinned and took another bite of his burger. He knew it might be a long shot, but he figured there was no harm in at least trying.

"I'm glad you asked. It's going to be boring and lonely. I could use some company. And if you don't believe in ghosts and don't spook easily, you shouldn't have any problems tagging along."

"What is it?" she asked, an interested look creeping across her face.

Cooper told her what he had planned, liking the idea even more when he pictured Stephanie being there with him.

"And you want me to come?" she asked after he told her.

"Absolutely."

Stephanie thought about it for a minute while she finished off her glass of wine. She looked to Cooper and then to the empty wine glass, considering.

"Fine," she said. "I'll go. But I'm going to need a few more of these."

EIGHT

As far as Cooper was concerned, the night was positively filled with small victories. Perhaps the most significant one came when they left the restaurant. Stephanie, never one to forfeit control of a situation and mostly distrustful of everyone—boyfriends, best friends, and parents included—handed Cooper her car keys as they walked into the parking lot. She'd had two more glasses of wine with dinner but was far from drunk, so she couldn't use that as an excuse.

Actually, she used no excuses. The simple fact of the matter was that Cooper knew where they were headed and she did not. He tried to tell himself that the small gesture meant nothing; it was just one person letting another person drive their car. But he also knew that it likely meant something else coming from Stephanie. A newfound sense of trust, perhaps? Or maybe it was nothing. Maybe it was just subconscious on her part.

Cooper pulled out of the restaurant lot and headed back down the main strip. He turned off of the main road six miles later as they entered the outskirts of Kill Devil Hills. He drove slowly down one of the more secluded beachfront neighborhoods and pointed to the house he had visited less than six hours ago.

"That's the Blackstock house," he said.

Stephanie looked out through the passenger window and made a *hmmph* sound.

"What?"

"Nothing. It's nice. Are they rich?"

"I don't think so. They do okay. That kind of family."

Stephanie shrugged, as if the topic didn't interest her anymore. "So, where is this place you're taking me?"

"Right up the road."

The spot he had in mind crept into view far sooner than he had expected. He hit the brakes and pulled off the road. There was no sort of access road or pavement to drive down or park on, so he settled for pulling just off the pavement and onto a small stretch of grit and sand along the side. With the car a good ten feet away from the road, he parked and killed the engine.

"I don't suppose you have a flashlight, do you?" Cooper asked.

"In the trunk. Why?"

"This is the place. A flashlight might come in handy. You never know."

"*This* is the place?" she asked suspiciously.

"Well, no. The place I was telling you about is just over this rocky little hill," he said, pointing directly to their right.

Cooper popped the trunk and got out of the car. When he opened the trunk and pulled the flashlight out of a small emergency kit tucked away in the corner, he could smell the ocean, salty and slightly fishy.

He checked the flashlight, saw that it supplied ample yellow-tinged light, and looked ahead to the rocky ground. He thought he'd save the batteries for later. After all, it might do Stephanie some good to have a little adventure in the dark—especially if he was trying to earn her trust all over again.

"Ready?" he asked

"Sure. Lead the way."

He walked toward the rockier ground ahead, enjoying the

knowledge that Stephanie was walking less than an arm's length away. The ground rose slightly, blocking off the view of the beach ahead of them. Yet as they neared the crest of the hill, Cooper heard the breaking waves. The sound was different at night. It was more muted, more droning. The air had the slightest nip to it, one of those that felt like a stubborn spring chill was clinging to it, refusing to accept that summer was on its heels.

They came to the top of the rocky terrain and stood motionless for a moment, looking out to the beach. It was secluded and dark, yet they could see everything. Their eyes had adjusted to the dark long before the beach had come into view and the moon was a generous three quarters full.

"It's pretty," Steph said.

"Yeah, it sort of is," Cooper replied.

"If I didn't know better, I'd think I was being set up for some sort of cheesy romantic gesture."

Cooper chuckled. "You and I both *wish* I could think that far ahead."

She shook her head, making a mocking noise and starting carefully down the hill. It was nearly a straight vertical drop of ten feet or so, the small rock face jagged and rough. Down near the sand, though, it smoothed out to a clean angle until the beach covered it. Steph did an excellent job of watching her footing and was down on the sand in less than five seconds.

Cooper remained at the top of the rocky hill. He stared out to his left and saw the two large black rocks that stuck up out of the water. Under the dark cover of night, the rocks looked like looming giants, something alive but remaining stationary to fool any unsuspecting prey.

"Is it the crabs?" Stephanie asked from below.

"What?"

"Crabs. They tend to scamper around on the beach at night from what I understand. You're hesitating up there. I figured you were scared of the crabs."

"No. I think I'll be okay."

Cooper tossed the flashlight down to her and made his way carefully down the shallow rock wall. Of course, the moment his feet touched the beach, he couldn't help but think of crabs scuttling across his feet with their little pincers snapping away.

"This way," Cooper said, walking toward the black rocks.

"Are those the rocks you think the kid was pointing to?" Stephanie asked.

"I don't know if he was pointing to them specifically. But he was pointing in this direction. And since those are the only definitive landmarks out here, it seems like the best spot."

"Why at night, though?"

"In just about every paranormal case I've ever been on, there's always more activity at night. Seems clichéd, I know. But that's just the way it is. It's usually best between one and four in the morning, but I figured you wouldn't want to stay awake that long."

Cooper came to a stop several feet away from the black stones. He was only inches away from where the waves crawled up onto the shore, little tendrils of water licking towards his feet.

Being so close to those rocks, he was able to truly appreciate their size. The one closest to the beach reached at least fifteen feet out of the water and into the air. It was jagged at the top but seemed to have softer edges on the way down until the sea covered it up. The second rock sat directly behind this one. Now that he was this close to them, Cooper thought that the two shapes might be part of the same rock formation, jutting out of the ocean floor but connected as one larger piece somewhere beneath the bottom.

Cooper sat down on the beach, mentally kicking himself for not bringing a towel. Then again, when he'd left his motel he hadn't thought that he'd be bringing Stephanie with him tonight. But she sat down on the sand next to him without complaint. She removed her flip flops and instantly stuck her toes into the sand, making tiny holes.

They sat that way for several minutes, not speaking, and staring out into the night-covered sea. Cooper didn't know why, but the sea at night spooked him a bit. During the day, there were the glittering caps and peaks to the water no matter how far out you looked. But at night, there were entire sections of the sea further out that looked to be pitch black, like the night sky was being devoured. It was easy to picture sea monsters and other unspeakable terrors lurking down there in the black depths.

That brought his attention back to the two large black rocks. He stared at them, watching how the water sloshed and violently crashed around their bases. Sea water churned between them, spitting up foam in sheets as the tide was interrupted and sucked between them.

"This silence isn't like us," Stephanie said.

The comment surprised Cooper. Not just because it broke his concentration from the rocks, but also because it was a very un-Stephanie thing to say.

"I agree," he said. "But I honestly don't know what to say. I feel like I need to apologize, but I'm not quite sure what I'd be apologizing for."

"Maybe for disappearing on me?"

"I really couldn't help that. I didn't *want* to disappear."

"Well, what about the four months between the last time you and I saw each other and the day you left for Kansas? What about that little period of time?"

She didn't seem angry, but the questions seemed barbed nonetheless. Stephanie had always had a very acute way of being able to ask painful and tricky questions in a harmless way. It had been infuriating when they were been dating and Cooper found it no less irritating now.

"I let work control me," he admitted. "I wanted to finish the new book ahead of schedule so I could take a month or so off to do absolutely nothing. If it helps, I wanted to take you with me to do that nothing."

After a moment of silence, she smiled thinly and said: "It helps a little."

"And then when I decided I was going to try this whole...*thing* with the Blackstocks, I knew you were the only person I could call. I felt like a jerk, calling you out of the blue like that. I really did. But I knew it had to be you...and I wanted to see you."

Stephanie considered this a bit as her eyes stared out into the watery darkness. "Are you sure this is what you want to do?"

"I don't know."

"I still don't understand what it is that you're trying to accomplish," she said. "All jokes aside, the way you explained it to me when you called, it sounds like you're setting out to be a ghostbuster or something."

"No, nothing like that. It's difficult to explain. When I came back from wherever I was, I started to get these really strange feelings deep down in my gut. I'd get them when I went online or read an article about the paranormal. These were the same sorts of things I was researching before my disappearance, but this time I had a different feeling about it. And when I read the story about the Blackstocks, I felt like something had kicked me in the stomach. The feeling of it, sort of like an aching pain on the inside, stayed around for days."

"So you think you're being...what? Summoned by something?"

Cooper stared out to the sea, watching a wave destroy itself and then inch up the shore. It stopped a few yards away from their feet and was pulled back out. He peered out to the darker folds and thought of

(*dark water*)

all of the monsters that could be lurking down there. He tried to come up with a suitable answer for Stephanie but couldn't find one that felt right.

"No, I don't think I'm being summoned," he said finally.

Then after some thought, he added: "Do you remember that exorcism case that shook me up so badly?"

"Yes. I explicitly remember it. I'd never seen you so scared before."

"And do you remember *why* I was so scared?"

She nodded and seemed to look back into time for a moment. "Because you said what you saw in that room changed your view on God. You started to believe in God that night and that scared you more than anything ever had. That sound about right?"

"That sounds perfect, actually," he said.

His mind raced back to the night in question. He could still see the young man, eighteen or nineteen years of age, laying in a hospital bed. Cooper had "spoken" to the evil presence in the man and had known full well that the doctors were out of clues and the man's psychologist was on the verge of giving up. Yet when an old preacher had come in with a Bible and started reading scripture and proclaiming the name of Christ, something had happened...something Cooper had not been prepared for. To think that such a power could exist within only a name had flipped many of his own beliefs—beliefs that had nothing at all to do with God or faith.

"This thing with the Blackstocks was sort of like that," Cooper said. "I don't know how to explain it. It wasn't a summoning but sort of how holy-rollers explain how God speaks to them. Something in their heart, or guts, or wherever."

"That sounds cheesy," Stephanie pointed out.

"Oh, I know. All I know is that when I got those two flashes in the Blackstock house today—the visions or whatever they were—it was confirmation. I'm supposed to be here. I'm supposed to be doing this."

"And you've never had visions before?"

"No. Well...there was that time I did peyote with that Native American tribe in Arizona. But I don't think that counts."

"Yeah, not so much. But not even after the exorcism? God didn't tap you on the shoulder with visions then?"

"I feel like you're making fun of me now."

"No. Just trying to understand."

Cooper felt another silence descending on them and didn't want to give it time to ruin the flow of conversation. So he opened his mouth and let the first thing on his mind come out.

"I missed you," he said. "I really think before all of this happened, we could have had a pretty good shot."

Stephanie tilted her head, considering. "Yeah, maybe."

"Maybe we *still* have a shot?"

His heart seemed to deflate as soon as he spoke the question into the air. He looked down, slightly embarrassed and very afraid. He watched her toes, still digging into the sand.

She smiled, but didn't look at him. "I think you need to get all of this sorted out first. I think you need to—"

She stopped there, as if looking for the right words. Once the quiet had reached an awkward lingering silence, Cooper looked away from her dirt-covered toes and to her face. She was looking towards the two large rocks, her eyes narrowed and inquisitive.

"What?" Cooper asked.

But then he followed her gaze and saw what had her so curious.

There was a human figure standing on top of the rock furthest out.

The shape was only slightly darker than the rock itself but stood out against the moonlit night fairly well. It was motionless, but was unmistakably a human figure. When Cooper had glanced out to the rocks less than a minute ago, it had not been there.

"You see it?" Stephanie asked in a whisper.

"Yeah."

"What is it? Is it a man?"

"I don't know."

Cooper slowly stood up, his eyes locked on the figure. He

shut his eyes tight for a moment and then opened them again. He wanted to make sure it wasn't simply the varying shades of black playing a trick on their eyes; the night, the rocks, and the figure itself created a dark yet distinguishable tapestry.

But the figure was still there.

And now it was moving.

It seemed to be shifting slowly to the edge of the rock, crawling down into the water. It moved with an eerie fluidity that Cooper had seen before. It was the movement of something that didn't have the physical restraints of flesh and bone.

"Cooper, that man wasn't there two or three minutes ago," Stephanie said. "And no one has come down the beach since we sat down."

"Yeah, I know."

He reached down and took the flashlight. He then took two steps forward but was stopped by Stephanie as she tugged at his jeans.

"What do you think you're doing?" she hissed.

"Going to check it out."

"Are you crazy?"

"Slightly. But what's it matter? It's just a person, right?"

"Did you see the way it moved?"

"I did. But you don't believe in ghosts. Remember?"

She didn't answer. She did, however, stand up with him. She stood very close to him and he noticed that her eyes showed a touch of concern.

"I never said I didn't believe," she said. "I said I was on the fence."

"Well then, come on down to the sand on my side." He gave her a nervous smile as he cut on the flashlight. "We've got some exploring to do."

NINE

When they were standing on the beach directly in front of the two large black rock outcroppings, the figure was no longer there. Its absence didn't matter, though. They had both seen it and even Stephanie, in her skeptical stubbornness, wasn't willing to say that it was just a trick of the night on their eyes. She had seen it; it had chilled her so badly that the hair on her arms was still standing on end.

In fact, as Cooper shone the flashlight onto the rocks, Stephanie seemed downright scared. Cooper, on the other hand, was used to these sorts of things. In the time he had spent working for the government and, more prominently, during the time he had worked on his own (much to the government's very vocal dismay), he had seen more than his fair share of anomalous events.

He had seen more than twenty of what he considered to be legitimate ghosts. He had seen a dozen UFOs, three of which had been less than fifty feet from the ground. He'd seen an old man levitate for five minutes and had seen a priest exorcise three demons from a teenager's body.

And that was just scratching the surface.

So a ghostly figure standing on top of a rock out at sea during the night didn't really spook him.

He had to admit, though…it was pretty cool.

He aimed the flashlight at the rock farthest out. The light didn't shine quite that far, so it barely illuminated it at all. Not only that, but the rock closest to them was catching most of the light and blocking it from its twin.

"Hold this, please," Cooper said, handing Stephanie the flashlight.

When she took it, he leaned down and started to roll up his pants legs. He had packed a few pairs of shorts but hadn't wanted to wear them out to dinner. And of course, there was no way he could have anticipated some late night water-wading when he'd gotten dressed.

He managed to roll his pants legs up to his knees with a little bit of effort and then took off his shirt. It wasn't until he had his shirt coming over his head that he realized that he was getting partially undressed in front of Stephanie. She'd seen him naked many times before, but he wasn't in the same shape now. These were depressing thoughts, but he was able to flush them out completely when he realized what he was about to do.

Priorities, Cooper…priorities.

He started walking towards the water but made it only two steps before Stephanie stopped him.

"What do you think you're doing?" she asked.

"I'm going to wade out and see if there's anyone there."

"That water is easily over your head. You really feel like going for a night swim?"

"Jenny Blackstock said that there are sandbars all over the place around here. Maybe I'll get lucky."

"And maybe you'll drown."

"Can you swim?" he asked her.

"Yes."

"Then come save me if you think I'm drowning. Do you want to keep the flashlight up here?"

She looked to the left and then to the right, discovering that there was no one else nearby. Much further down to the right, back towards the Blackstock house, a man was walking a dog but he was headed in the other direction and was little more than a speck in the dark distance.

"Yeah," Stephanie said. "If you don't mind, leave the light with me. Just please hurry up and be careful."

He nodded and started walking out into the water. It was much chillier than he remembered from earlier in the day when he had stuck his feet in. It took his breath for a moment, but it wasn't entirely unpleasant.

He waded out in the water up to his knees and had to put forth a little effort to push against the small, oncoming waves. He kept going out, the water now up to his thighs. After several more short steps, he began to feel the sludgy sand beneath his feet start to rise. It was a very gradual rise but within just two more steps forward, he realized that he had come to one of the sandbars that Jenny had mentioned. He walked further out, rising up out of the water little by little. The sandbar leveled out and he found himself in water up to his calves.

He looked back to Stephanie and gave her a thumbs up. Even in the darkness, he could sense her eye-rolling. She pointed the flashlight in his direction, but it did little good. When he turned back toward the rocks—the first one now no more than a dozen or so feet away—he peered out to the abyss-like darkness of the sea ahead. He cringed, not liking the idea of any of his body in that water even if it *was* just his feet.

He looked away from that darkness and stared directly in front of him. A bit of the flashlight's soft beam could be seen in the water ahead, so he followed it. Stephanie was keeping it aimed directly in front of him, tracing out a path to the rocks. He kept his eyes on the point where the beam faded out, flush against the side of the first rock. The sandbar remained level and he was able to cover the few feet with no problem.

When he reached the first large rock, he peered up its side

and thought he could possibly climb it if he had to. But if this sandbar remained level, he thought he could likely just walk around it and directly to the second rock, where they had seen the figure.

"Anyone out here?" he called out.

His only response was the soft slushing of water around the base of the rocks and the gentle crashing of small nighttime waves.

He walked to the right in order to slink around the first rock and felt the sandbar drop off. There was no gradual decline to the sand, but a complete drop. He realized this too late. His right foot went plunging off the sandbar and, when he reached out to the first rock to catch his balance, he fell over.

He went under the water for a moment and, when he popped back up, he was ashamed to realize that he had been utterly terrified when he had gone down. He set his feet down, found the ocean floor, and stood. The floor beneath his feet was rocky— part of the large rocks that loomed over him to the left, he assumed. The water was now up to his shoulders and he had to stand on his tiptoes to prevent water from slapping him in the face and going into his mouth.

"Are you okay?" Stephanie called out from behind him.

"Yeah," he said, spitting out salty sea water. "Ran out of sandbar."

He reached out to the left and found the surface of the first rock. When he pulled himself around to the back of it, he found an empty space between the rocks that was much smaller than he had expected when he had viewed them from the beach earlier in the day. Behind the first rock, it almost looked as if the rocks overlapped beneath the water. He also saw that the water flowing between the rocks swirled in a weird little pool before finally escaping the stone's clutches and continuing its journey to shore.

Using a slippery grip on the first rock and the awkward bobbing of his feet to guide him, Cooper waded over to the space between the stones. He felt the hard rocky surface of one of the rocks beneath his feet, but wasn't sure which rock he was standing on. One thing he *was* certain of, though, was that the current of water that ran between the two rocks was incredibly strong. Something about the positioning of the rocks create a sort of suction that gave that particular current of water more power. He held tightly to the side of the first rock and still had to firmly plant his legs to not get swept away.

He wasn't sure why, but something about the way the water flowed into that little pool between that small V-shaped space between the rocks seemed strange. He had no doubt that, if he were to let go of the side of the rock, it would easily sweep him through the space between the rocks. He then wondered if someone could get stuck between them and drown if the tide got high enough.

Those are stupid thoughts to be having right now, he thought.

He looked to the second rock and was pretty sure he could make it over there without the water sweeping him off to the other side of the rocks. But really, what was the point? If there had been a person up there earlier, what was he going to do? Swim after them and ask what they were up to?

Hardly.

Besides, if his hunch was correct—if what they had spotted was a ghost or spirit or something similar—going to that second rock to find it was futile.

Defeated, wet, and with legs that were growing tired from fighting the tide, Cooper figured it was time to go back. If there was something to be found here, he wasn't going to find it at night, anyway.

He turned back, already anxious for the relief the sandbar would provide. But as he made his first sluggish stride away from the side of the rock, he heard something that caught his attention.

It was slight, buried beneath the sloshing noise of the water that churned between the rocks. At first, he thought it was nothing and nearly ignored it. But once he heard it, it was hard to *not* hear it.

It sounded like someone pouring water into a bowl, only denser. It was hard to tell where it was coming from, but he thought it was directly beside him.

He lunged back to the backside of the rock, catching himself along the edge. He scaled the side of the larger rock and went to the back of it. The water between the rocks sucked at him, trying to pull him away, but he clung steadfast to the slick handholds along the surface. He looked down to where the water was splashing against the side of the rock and thought he saw the source of the sound.

In the dark, it was impossible to tell for sure, but he *thought* there was an anomaly there.

Curious, Cooper splashed back out into the water and, with two labored strokes, made it back to the sandbar. He stood there for a moment and caught his breath. He then looked to Stephanie and held up a hand.

"I need the flashlight," he called out to her. "Can you throw it this far?"

She looked at the flashlight, considering. He knew she wasn't wondering whether or not she could get it to him (she was stronger than he was when it came to arm strength), but whether or not she wanted to part with it. After a few seconds, she cocked her arm back and threw it in a perfect underhanded arc to him. Her aim was dead on and he caught it with no problem.

He turned to the rocks and saw that they looked slimy with the flashlight's beam directly upon them. Holding the flashlight up over his head, Cooper walked back off the sandbar. He was ready for the drop this time and managed to keep his head above the water.

As he directed the light around the rocks, he got a very brief sense of familiarity—of venturing into uncertain places where any form of danger might be around the corner. Although his relationship with the FBI and the shadow organizations, that had later sought him out, had spoiled him and left him disenchanted over his career, he couldn't deny that he had loved it. He felt a slight pang of regret over his past as he stood neck deep in the water, skimming the flashlight along the base of the two large rocks ahead of him.

Having only one free hand this time, it was harder to grab onto the first rock. He stretched his arm out and managed to dig into a sizable crevice with his fingers. He pulled himself forward and shuffled his feet blindly under the water for some sort of foot hold. He found one and managed to pull himself up a bit as he climbed around to the rear side of the rock yet again.

He shone the flashlight into the V-shaped region of water between the rocks, looking for the source of the pouring sound. Now that he couldn't *unhear* it, he thought it sounded like rain water channeling down through a city drain. Only this drain would be very deep, and the water was much stronger than simple rain spillage.

With the flashlight, it was easy to find the source. Roughly three inches above where the water was currently splashing against the rock, there was a large crack that was taking in water. The crack was about the size of a soccer ball and was located along a curve in the rock that made it hard to spot. If the tide was just a bit higher, Cooper would not have been able to hear the sound, much less spot the crack.

Pressing the flashlight against the side of the rock, Cooper managed to angle himself over to his right in order to get closer to it. His footing slipped a few times in the muck along the submerged base of the rock but he somehow kept his head from going under.

He was now facing the hole and was able to place his fingers along its sides. As he pulled himself up by it, he fought against the surging water between the rocks. He aimed the flashlight into the hole and saw nothing. There was only blackness, but it was not the solid shade of black that made up the rest of the rocks, made darker by the constant beating of the sea and the shade of night.

No, he was fairly certain that he was looking into a deep, dark hole.

He could hear water splashing down inside of it. The sound it made led him to believe that the hole (if that's what it was) was rather deep.

He leaned closer into it and gave a fairly loud *"Hello!"*

His voice reverberated and produced a slight echo. Combined with the water, it was difficult to tell just what was going on in there. He felt around along the steep angled face of the rock, looking for small stones but found only slime and grit.

Knowing that there was a good chance that he'd promptly regret the decision to do so, Cooper cut off the flashlight and popped open the tab on the end of it. Doing this required two hands and he nearly slid right off of the rock and into the water. He pressed himself into the rock as he worked though, making sure he stayed tight to it.

He slid the batteries out of the flashlight and palmed them in his hand. He selected one and dropped it into the hole. Leaning forward, he listened as closely as he could and started making a silent count in his head. He did his best to shut out the sound of the tide and the waves crashing on the shore.

One, two, three—

He heard the battery clatter off something but sensed that it had not come to a complete stop.

—four, five, six—

He heard the battery hit something else. This time the sound was more solid. Cooper was pretty sure it had hit bottom. He wasn't certain what this meant, but his mind returned to the fact that, on the other side of the beach, closer to the road and where they had parked Stephanie's car, the ground was rocky and uneven in most places.

It made him wonder just how expansive the open spaces beneath this rock might be.

"Cooper?"

Stephanie's voice was remarkably clear over the sounds of the sloshing water between the rocks and the waves. He carefully inched his way along the side of the rock, carrying the now useless flashlight in his left hand. He got to the side of the rock and looked out to her. With no light source and no way to really investigate the hole at night, he figured it was time to head back, anyway.

But then he saw her face. Even in the muted moonlight, he could see that she was scared.

She was frightened and she was pointing directly at him.

No, not at him.

Behind him.

Cooper turned his head, not daring to let go of the side of the rock.

A man stood on the second rock behind Cooper. Only, to call it a man was being far too polite.

The figure's face was rotten, the skin mottled, black and barely there. It also had no eyes, only black sockets. When it grinned maliciously at Cooper, the figure revealed teeth that were nothing more than brown shapes that resembled wood.

Cooper had seen a lot during his career, but never this up-close.

And despite all of his experience, Cooper could not help himself.

He screamed.

TEN

The scream that came out of Cooper's mouth sounded strange to him. After all he had seen in his line of work, it took a lot to frighten him. He had developed something of a tolerance for fear. But this gruesome figure had come out of nowhere and was standing less than three feet away.

Only, the man wasn't standing.

There was no way for the figure to firmly plant its feet on the sloped surface of the second rock. From what Cooper could tell, the man was floating or, more likely, he was not a man at all. In a dizzying moment, Cooper was quite sure the figure's left foot had dissolved into the rock, passing right through it.

It took Cooper less than two seconds to take all of this in. He finished his scream by allowing his fear to also control his hands and feet. He released the rock and went into the water. The current between the rocks caught him at once, tugging him hard to the right. He let it take him and, when it pulled him under, he swam furiously until he felt the push of the tide, carrying him towards the shore. Cooper then realized that he was now on the opposite side of the rocks and that the sandbar was nowhere to be found. He swam with the tide and did not stop swimming until he could fully place his feet on the bottom.

As he managed to stand back up, he could still feel the undertow tugging at him. He lost his footing and went under, but he continued to crane his head back as he looked for the figure on the second rock. All he saw, though, was the water as it went over his head. He took in a mouthful of salt water and started coughing and gagging as he tried to swim towards the beach.

When the next series of waves came surging forward, he caught the current and swam with it again. He kept stroking forward until he felt his knees dragging on soft dirt. He then stood up and ambled the rest of the way to the beach, still coughing up sea water.

He turned back to the rocks and was not at all surprised to see that the eyeless figure, that had so badly scared him, was no longer there.

Stephanie came running to him as he went to his butt in the sand. Between the exercise of maneuvering around the rocks, the genuine scare, and then fighting against the current to get back to shore, Cooper was beyond winded.

"Are you okay?" Stephanie asked.

He gave her a thumbs-up as he coughed up more sea water. He wasn't sure he'd ever get it all up. Again, he looked back out to the rocks, hoping that they might offer up their secrets again.

"Cooper, what was that? What did I just see?"

"I don't know. A ghost, for sure. But I don't know which kind."

"There's more than one kind of ghost?"

"Yeah. Intelligent, residual, poltergeist, and demonic entity." The words came out like harsh whispers as his throat ached form all the coughing.

"And which was that?"

"Are you telling me you believe in ghosts now?"

Stephanie looked to the rocks and shrugged her shoulders nervously. "Cooper, the man—or ghost or whatever it was— was *floating*. I didn't even see his feet. So yeah, I'm off the fence now. Smack dab in the mud and cow patties on your side."

"Welcome," Cooper said after one last cough. "As for that ghost, I don't know which kind it was. Pretty sure it wasn't demonic. But it's impossible to tell for sure without knowing more about the location."

"You think it's related to the Blackstocks?"

"It would be *really* coincidental if it wasn't."

Stephanie was still looking out to the rocks. Cooper saw that she was trembling slightly. And, even in the gentle darkness of night, he could see that she was slightly pale. He didn't think any of it it was because she was cold.

"Did you see its face?" Cooper asked.

"Not really."

"Good."

He stood up, realizing that he still had her flashlight in his hand. He offered it back to her and she took it as if she had never seen it before. Cooper was beginning to wonder if she was in some sort of minor shock. She clicked the button to turn it on but nothing happened.

"Sorry," he said. "I lost a battery."

"How?"

"Doing an experiment."

She laughed ironically and said, "And did you find out anything?"

"I don't know. There's a crack in the rock—a small hole that I couldn't really see into. I'm pretty sure those rocks are part of the exterior to a tunnel or cave system that run under the beach."

"Can you tell me about it somewhere else? Quite frankly, I'm ready to get the hell out of here."

"Yeah. I can't really do much about this at night anyway."

"You mean you're not done?" she asked, clearly shocked. "After coming face to face with that...*thing*, you're going to keep looking?"

"Of course."

He then placed his arm around her shoulders and escorted her back towards the small rocky hill they had come down to reach the beach. She stepped closer, leaning into him. They headed back to the car like that, Cooper's arm around her as they walked as closely together as their bodies would allow.

Despite the adrenaline and fear still surging through him, Cooper noticed that she was not shying away from him. In her own fear, she was seeking his comfort.

Another small victory, Cooper thought as they climbed back up the little hill and walked to her car.

ELEVEN

It was shortly after eleven o'clock when Cooper pulled Stephanie's car back into the restaurant parking lot. They made the drive with the windows rolled down, trying to dry Cooper's pants as much as possible. Stephanie made him sit on a hooded sweatshirt she had taken from the trunk of her car, not wanting him to soak her seat.

Cooper pulled the car into the spot beside his own but didn't get out right away. He looked over to Stephanie and saw that whatever shock she had been creeping towards on the beach was gone now. He assumed that also meant that whatever lapse in her guard she had encountered afterwards—allowing him to put his arm around her and comfort her—was also gone.

"Are you going to be okay?" he asked her.

"Yeah. I think so."

"Do you need me to come back to your room with you?"

She gave him a playfully disappointed look and shook her head. "Well played, but no thanks."

"Can't blame a guy for trying."

"No, I can't," she said. She then leaned over slowly and gave him a kiss on the cheek.

"Thanks for coming out with me tonight," Cooper said. "To dinner *and* to the beach. Sorry you got such a scare."

"It's okay. I'm glad I saw it. I kind of understand why you've always been so fascinated with this sort of stuff now."

"I don't know that *fascinated* is the right word."

"Whatever word you want to use…that sight is going to stick with me for a while."

"So how about tomorrow?" Cooper asked. "You want to lend a hand?"

"If I can. Remember, I'm leaving tomorrow afternoon. Sometime around four."

"I know. And don't forget, I still get one more question from dinner."

"Sure. I'll call you tomorrow morning."

He wanted to stay, to create the opportunity to talk more. He especially wanted to explore what she was thinking now that she had seen something undeniably supernatural up close and personal. But he knew Stephanie; if she wanted to talk about it, she would. He wasn't about to pressure her after having been away from her for so long. He figured it was best to offer her complete control over the flow and timing of their friendship and anything that might come out of it.

In that moment, he also thought about his jarring experience in a hospital room several years ago, watching a priest peacefully reading from a Bible while a young man screamed in a voice that was not his own. It had taken that moment to totally flip Cooper's beliefs about God. It had been unexpected, and he'd spent several weeks trying to process it. In all honesty, he wasn't sure if he'd ever fully processed it.

He wondered if that was how Stephanie was feeling about the supernatural right now. If so, he felt for her. It was invasive and, in a way, extremely private at the same time.

Cooper got out of the car before any gut-wrenching tension could bloom between them. He gave her a wave, which she returned with a smile as she slid across to the driver's seat. He then got into his own car and waited until she pulled out and turned onto the main strip.

He watched her go and then sat in the parking lot for a while, too amped to go even think about returning to his room to go to sleep.

COOPER'S first instinct was to go back to the spot along the road where he had parked Stephanie's car an hour and a half ago. He wouldn't go down to the beach, just to the edge of the small rock wall they had climbed down. He could sit there for a while and see if the figure reappeared.

And if it did...well, he'd figure it out as it happened. That was usually how he worked in situations like this.

But that plan seemed like a waste of time. It was too dark outside and he had no equipment. The old Cooper would have a trunk full of technological gadgets to record and analyze the phenomenon. With none of that at his disposal, there were only his instincts and, apparently, the weird new power he'd used at the Blackstock residence.

He assumed the power was some sort of ability to have visions. He'd been aware of it just as soon as he had reappeared nine months ago. He'd sensed it here and there, like a strange kind of deja vu. He'd known *something* was there but had never dared test it. Besides, it had never been as powerful as it had been on the Blackstocks's front porch. Besides...even if his new abilities *did* have something to show him out on those black rocks, he was pretty sure he didn't want to see it.

As he finally pulled out of the restaurant parking lot and hit the main strip, Cooper found himself missing the old version of himself. It was a younger, cockier version that feared nothing and would walk into the darkness with a pack stuffed with thermal guns, audio recorders and an assortment of other devices. Things had made sense then. The uncertainty of the future had served as its own mystery, just as promising as the hope of unlocking some new paranormal puzzle.

But now the unknown was a frightening monster lurking around the corner. The questions he had now were beyond the realm of the merely supernatural. They now went somewhere much deeper than he was ready to explore.

He'd been more confident about *everything* back then. And, although it had only been a little less than half a year ago, it was beginning to feel like he'd been living an entirely different life as the Cooper M. Reid of old. He'd been over-confident with his work, sure, but that was because he was extremely good at it. It had taken his disappearance to clue him in to the fact that, if he'd continued along that road, someone in the government would have *had* to shut him up before all was said and done.

If he'd continued down that road prior to the disappearance, it would have ended in death. It was a fact he'd ignored and avoided at all costs before, but now seemed crystal clear.

He'd seen the seedier bowels of the FBI, CIA, and other government agencies that didn't even have proper names. He knew that killing some snooping little writer and struggling former agent was not a concern at all. No one would blink an eye, even if that corpse had once been a very accomplished FBI asset and cult pop-culture icon.

For that very reason, there was currently no equipment in Cooper's trunk. All he carried from his old life was a Sig Sauer P226 that he kept beneath the driver's seat. It had been the gun he'd carried while an agent for the FBI and the shadow organization that he had worked under for several years afterwards. He'd become quite good with the Sig and had gone to great lengths to get one before coming out to North Carolina. He had no idea what the first step of his bizarre life had in store, but he felt a little more comfortable knowing that the familiar feel of the Sig was within his reach.

With no equipment and no real clues of any kind, Cooper figured it was time to start doing some digging. His laptop was back at the motel and, as much as he hated to confine himself to his motel room with such a huge reserve of energy within him, he thought it might be the smartest thing to do.

He traveled the main strip along the primary businesses one last time. As midnight neared, most of them were closing up shop. A few neon lights blazed in bar windows and cheap souvenir shops, but the strip was basically dead. He thought about Stephanie and how he was beginning to feel that, if there was anything at all left from their previous relationship, it was buried it deep. He knew from experience that she was great at hiding her feelings and no amount of chivalry or romantic gestures would cause her to dig them back up. She'd always been distant and guarded with a rough exterior. That hadn't seem to have changed much since he'd last seen her, and he didn't see any real progress happening anytime soon.

For now, he'd just have to make do with the small victories as they came to him.

Ten minutes later, he returned to his motel room—a small, bland square of a room that seemed to contain objects that were just as square and bland: the soap, the sink, the TV, the dresser, the bed. He showered just to get the salt from the ocean out of his hair, threw on some clothes, and plopped himself down behind his laptop. Using the motel's slow WiFi connection, he did some research into the area just outside of Kill Devil Hills.

He sat in front of the screen for an hour. The light from his laptop was the only illumination in the room. The first thing to come up when doing research into the area was the Wright Brothers and their first flight. Wrapped up in his own little mystery, Cooper had nearly forgotten that the history of American flight had gotten its start just a few miles down the road. But once he got more keyword-specific with his search, he started to find more of what he was looking for.

He jotted a few notes down in a notepad—one of a few remaining habits from his time as a hotshot author—but wasn't making any connections. He started to form a few good ideas that he thought might lead somewhere but, by the time things started connecting for him, he was starting to grow tired. Perhaps, he thought, it would be easier to put it all together after a couple hours of sleep.

As he started to shut the computer down, he was startled by a soft knock at the door.

He stared at the door for a moment, uncertain. Had someone from the government found him already? Maybe they knew he had returned and had somehow tracked him down. He knew he'd been careful in making sure he'd covered all of his bases, double and triple-checking his methods. But he knew the lengths that some of those he had once worked for might go to in order to get what they wanted.

And if they wanted him quiet, they'd get it one way or the other.

Maybe now was the time that he would be taken out behind some abandoned building and shot in the back of the head.

The knock came again.

He imagined some goon in a black suit, looking like the fabled Men in Black. Only this Man in Black would care nothing about UFOs or extraterrestrial activity. He'd simply put a bullet between Cooper's eyes, dispose of the body (probably in a beach drainage ditch somewhere nearby) and then head back to the shadowed corners of whatever secret organization had sent him.

The knock came again, a little more insistent this time.

As Cooper inched towards the door, he cursed at himself for leaving his gun in the car. He approached the door and peeked through the peephole, prepared to see the worst.

A burden lifted from his heart instantly, allowing it to soar when he saw Stephanie on the other side. He unlocked the door, unfastened the chain lock at the top, and opened it.

"Hey," she said. She looked tired and a little embarrassed.

"Hey," Cooper echoed.

"I couldn't sleep."

"I'm sorry."

A thought occurred to him then—one that had tickled at his mind before dinner but he had never gotten around to. "How did you know where I was staying?"

She sighed sleepily. "I booked the room for you, Cooper. Remember?"

"Yeah. That's right. Sorry."

"Can I sleep here?"

"Of course." Cooper moved to the side of the doorway to let her enter.

She was carrying a small backpack over her shoulder, and was dressed in a white tee shirt and a pair of athletic shorts. Her hair was a bit of a mess and she wasn't wearing makeup. She looked cute, like a teen girl headed to a sleepover. He smiled at her as she made her way to the queen-sized bed even though it was clear she wasn't in a smiling mood.

Stephanie went straight to the bed and sprawled out, wasting no time trying to recapture her sleep.

"Cooper?"

"Yeah?"

"I'd like for you to sleep beside me," she said. Her voice was quiet and a bit shaky. "I'm sort of creeped out. But please don't make me regret getting you a room with just one bed."

Cooper wasn't quite sure how to take that comment, so he simply said "Okay."

He went into the bathroom to brush his teeth and, by the time he came back out, Stephanie was under the covers. He didn't think twice about it when he closed his laptop lid and lay down beside her, making sure not to infringe upon her space.

He settled in quietly, enjoying the feel of her weight on the other side of the bed. He listened to her breathing for a while, wondering if he should even *try* to scoot over and put an arm around her. It had been almost two years (maybe a little longer; he honestly had trouble putting together the pieces of time) since they'd shared a bed and, back then, it had been *very* different.

"Cooper?" she asked in the darkness.

"Yeah?"

"I need to ask you something, but after you answer, we forget that this night ever happened. Can you agree to that?"

It felt like a trap, a cleverly worded snare. "I guess."

"Do you think we would have ever worked out?"

Stephanie rarely asked questions like this. Like Cooper, she wasn't much for sentiment. Such a question coming from her was a huge deal. He understood this and did his best to remain calm and honest as he answered. He also knew that he had to give a good answer because he'd likely not get this opportunity again.

"I think so," he said. "It was my fault. I was stupid. My priorities were messed up."

"I agree wholeheartedly. But was it worth it? In the end—after your disappearance and everything—was throwing what we had away worth it?"

It wasn't an easy answer, so he did the best he could. "I don't know yet," he said truthfully. "Until I can figure out where the hell I was for three whole months, that's not a question I can answer."

"I missed you," she said. "When I heard your voice on the phone after all that time, I had to use every ounce of strength in me not to cry on the spot. It sounds like an obvious thing to say, but I was really glad you hadn't died. And honestly, I think, somewhere in my stupid head, I always assumed you hadn't. Isn't that weird?"

He didn't answer. He let it all sink in, wishing things could be different and hating himself a little.

"For what it's worth," she added, "I think we could have made it work, too."

They were quiet for another thirty seconds or so. Cooper slowly started rolling his body over, determined that he would, at the very least, hold her.

"Cooper?" she said, her voice so soft it was nearly a whisper.

"Yeah?"

"One more thing."

"What's that?"

"If you come over on my side of the bed, I'm going to knee you in the boy-parts."

He laughed quietly, although he knew she was serious. He'd treated her badly and he deserved her defensive attitude. Even if he had treated her like a queen, his job had always come first and that wasn't fair. He knew this without a doubt and had never argued that she was wrong whenever she'd mentioned it in the past.

His work and reputation had always come first. Some ambitious journalist once referred to him as *"the Hunter S. Thompson of the paranormal"* and Cooper had done everything he could to live up to it. And now, although what he was doing wasn't really work, it was still taking top priority over everything else.

Including Stephanie. Again.

Still, she'd agreed to help him and had even faced something sinister tonight as a result. And she was still here with him, lying beside him and trusting him.

He really didn't deserve her...not in *any* capacity.

He was going to ask her something about possibly trying to make things work again but her light snoring put a stop to it. He looked over at her and smiled.

He listened to her little snores and closed his eyes. Within five minutes, he was snoring right alongside her, the merest trace of a smile still lingering at the corner of his mouth.

TWELVE

They had a cheap breakfast of donuts and coffee at a small coffee shop looking out onto the beach. They sat in patio chairs, enjoying the morning breeze and the sight of the sun on the sea. Gulls sailed and looped and dove down over the shore, as if aware they had an audience.

As they ate, they looked over the few notes Cooper had compiled the night before. He was glad that Stephanie was there to look over the list with him. She had a great way of making him realize when his ideas were fruitless, something he'd resented at one point in their past. But now he was able to see the benefit of it. It kept him grounded and centered on the matter at hand. It was all a part of her tough love and honesty.

In a very odd way, it's what he had missed the most about her.

After looking over his list for twenty seconds, Stephanie pointed to a single word. She left a smear of jelly filling from her donut on the paper.

"I think that's your ticket right there," she said.

The word she had pointed to was *caves.*

"It's really the only thing I can think of," Cooper agreed. "I don't even know how it might relate to the figure on the rocks, but I definitely heard water pouring down into something deep. And it took that flashlight battery a long time to drop."

"Do you even know if there are any caves around this area?"

"Not that I could see. But the little bit of digging I did revealed that sometime back in the early 1700s, there was some pirate activity in the area. There was a fight between two pirate crews over some gold or something. There were a few pirate crews that tended to hide in these tight little coves and caverns that led out to sea."

"For real? Like *Pirates of the Caribbean*-type pirates?"

"That's the lamest pirate metaphor ever. But yes. Real pirates with the hats and the eye patches and the beards. Maybe even peg legs and parrots, who knows? I read a story on one of the historical society sites about how there were these underground chambers scattered all along the coast where it was rumored that the pirates hid their gold."

Stephanie was grinning at him, but it was not in a totally joking manner. "You're not just making this up so we can go off looking for buried treasure, are you?"

"No. After seeing that thing up so close and personal last night, treasure is the last thing on my mind. Besides, I don't think there's going to be any gold or treasure at the end of this story."

"Have you decided if you're going to tell the Blackstocks?"

"Not yet," he answered, though it was something that likely needed to be addressed. "Right now, I don't see the point. It's useless to tell them that we saw something that was very likely a ghost near a site their son was pointing to just before he died. It wouldn't do anything to ease their pain. If anything, it would probably make things worse."

He took a moment to appreciate what this meant. In the past, he probably would have wasted no time in mentioning such a thing to grieving parents. Back then, he would have done just about anything to push things along to some sort of powerful climax. It made for good entertainment, a point of great interest in his next book.

Stephanie popped the remainder of her donut into her mouth and looked at his list again. "You know, I thought someone that wrote about this stuff at one point in his life would take better notes than this."

"I'm trying to not be that guy anymore."

"How's that going for you?"

"It's harder than I thought."

"But you're sure this is what you're supposed to be doing now?"

"Pretty sure, yeah."

"Is this certainty tied to your visions?" she asked. "Do you feel like you're being *led* to help the Blackstocks?"

He offered a grin, both amused and slightly aggravated by how she continued to challenge him. "I do," he said.

"Led by who or what?" she asked. "God, maybe?"

"Maybe." He was about to go on but then stopped with his mouth still slightly open. "Hold on. How about you? Do you even believe in God?"

At that, Stephanie stood up and offered her hand, shrugging the question off. "Let's get out of here and go find some treasure."

"All the treasure was recovered and divvied up between museums," Cooper said, taking her offered hand and standing up anyway.

"You're a buzzkill, Cooper. I guess you really *are* changing."

STEPHANIE DROVE THIS TIME, taking them back to the place along the beach they had visited the night before. She parked in the exact same spot and they walked out onto the rocky terrain, finding that it looked totally different in the light of day. They could hear waves crashing, gulls crying and, somewhere in the distance, the droning of a lawn mower.

The noise of the ocean seemed to call to them, almost like it was teasing them with the horror it had tossed out to them the night before. But as they walked, they were more interested in the rocky ground at their feet. They walked along strategically, Stephanie fanning out to the right and Cooper marching along to the left, looking down to the ground for any obvious fissures or other indications of a cave beneath their feet.

There wasn't much ground to cover to either side. On the left, further away from the beach houses and the town beyond, a few small dunes and crabgrass took over. To the right, there were sporadic weeds and the occasional beige indication of sand beneath it. From the spot where the car was parked to the slight drop off onto the beach (which didn't look nearly as tall in the daylight) the area covered about one hundred feet.

"Anything?" Cooper asked after about fifteen minutes of searching.

"Nothing," Stephanie answered. "Just rocks and bird crap."

"Let's check the little cliff," Cooper said, pointing towards the beach.

They walked to the edge and ambled down with much more grace than they had displayed nine hours ago. The rock face seemed sturdier as it was warmed by the morning sun. When they were both on the sand below, they studied the small rock wall that separated the rocky terrain from the beach. It took less than five minutes of searching to discover that other than a few minor nooks and crannies, there was nothing of interest.

"So what does this mean?" Stephanie asked.

"It means that, if there *are* caves around here, the entrances to them have probably been sealed up."

"So more research is in our future?"

"Yeah. Hooray."

Cooper walked a few yards further down towards the water and looked to the two big black rocks to the left. He then looked to his right, in the direction of the beach houses. There were a few people out, skirting along the shoreline. Two younger boys were waist deep in the water carrying body boards, far enough away to be nothing more than splashing smudges in the water.

"This all looks very different in the day, doesn't it?" Cooper said.

"Yeah," she said sarcastically. "I think it's because of the sun."

"No, I mean...well, I don't know what I mean. It *feels* different. Houses that are legitimately haunted sometimes feel the same way. They feel mostly fine and normal during the day but then you can actually feel the sinister vibe of the place once night falls."

"And you're getting that here, on this beach?"

"Not very strong...but there's *something*. You don't feel it?"

He was surprised to see that she was actually taking the time to concentrate. Of course, her eyes were hiding behind her sunglasses, so he couldn't see her reaction. But she stayed that way for a good ten seconds before she shrugged in defeat.

"I don't know," she said. "I'm not sure what I'm supposed to be feeling, I guess."

Cooper was about to explain it to her when he noticed someone walking in their direction. It was a woman, walking toward them from the direction of the beach houses. At first, he thought it was Jenny Blackstock but then realized that this woman was shorter and had a darker shade of blonde hair.

Stephanie followed his gaze and gave the woman a polite smile.

"Do you know her?" she asked Cooper quietly.

"No."

The woman was edging closer to them, angling away from the ocean and directly towards them. She was close enough to limit any further hushed conversation, close enough for Cooper to see that she was an older lady and her eyes were blue.

"Hello there," the woman said.

"Hi," Cooper and Stephanie said, nearly in unison.

Now that she was closer to them, Cooper thought that this woman was likely in her late fifties—at least fifteen years older than Jenny Blackstock. She was well-tanned and carried the vibe of someone that was happy most of the time. Her smile seemed genuine and the cheer in her voice was thick.

"I'm so sorry to intrude," she said, looking directly at Cooper. "But at the risk of seeming like a nosy old biddy, I believe you were out here yesterday with the Blackstocks. Is that correct?"

"Yes," Cooper said hesitantly. "Can I ask how you know that?"

The woman pointed back the way she had come. "I live in the last house on the row. I saw you from my kitchen window yesterday and sort of snooped a bit. So I guess I really *am* something of a nosy old biddy. I watched you walk all the way out here with them. And then I saw you hopping down off the rock wall a few minutes ago while I was on my back porch, having my morning coffee."

Cooper glanced at the house, sitting about one hundred yards away. He tried to imagine living in a house where you could see the two large black rocks from your back porch. A chill passed through him like a rocket.

"That probably sounded stalker-like," the woman said. "I apologize. I also apologize for prying, but there's really no way to subtly ask this next question. But…were you talking to them about the weird things that happen around their house?"

Cooper was quickly growing uncomfortable with the conversation and hoped that Stephanie would intervene with her quick wit. But she remained silent, maybe enjoying the sight of him being taken off guard.

Or maybe just as equally thrown off by the odd vibe this woman was causing.

"I don't think the Blackstocks would want me divulging that information," Cooper said.

"Probably not," the woman agreed.

Cooper looked to Stephanie, giving her a quick *help me out* face.

The woman frowned and extended her hand. "Please forgive me," she said. "My name is Mary Guthrie. Like I said, I live right there in the very last house on this stretch. And if you *were* here talking to the Blackstocks about the things that go on in their house, I think I might have some things to add."

"Like what?" Cooper asked, not realizing until it was too late that he had basically showed his hand with the question.

"It depends. Are they hearing the laughter of children at night?"

Cooper's discomfort vanished in an instant, replaced with curiosity. He noticed that Stephanie went rigid beside him. She took a slow step away from Mary Guthrie.

"How did you know that?" Cooper asked.

Mary smiled and tilted her head back towards her house. "Tell me," she said. "What exactly is it that you do? Why are you here to see the Blackstocks?"

"I'm just trying to help."

"Are you one of those ghost hunters or something?"

"No. Not exactly. I'm just here to help."

"Do you know *how* to help them?"

"No," Cooper admitted, starting to get annoyed with Mary Guthrie's questions.

"Why don't you come with me?" Mary asked. "I think I might have something you'd want to see."

THIRTEEN

They followed Mary Guthrie back to her house, Stephanie walking closely to Cooper as they got better acquainted with the woman. Cooper glanced back only a single time to take in the sight of the two black rocks. Part of him fully expected the rocks to be moving with them, keeping pace. It was just a funny sort of vibe he was starting to pick up—a vibe that he had come to know and trust during his careers as an FBI agent and a writer.

After formal introductions were made—Cooper being as vague as he could about his history and identity—he warmed up to Mary Guthrie a bit. Even in her countless apologies about seeming like a snoop, there was an aura of good cheer about her.

"So do you live here during the summer?" Cooper asked.

"No. I'm leaving next week to go to my summer home in Massachusetts. I've already got this house rented out through the end of August with only one week left open."

"But you live here for the rest of the year?"

"From the end of September to the beginning of June," Mary said. "The beach is so much nicer when it's quiet and all of the tourists have packed up and gone home." She grinned politely and added: "No offense."

"None taken."

Stephanie remained quiet, which struck Cooper as odd. Usually, she was extremely talkative around new people, wanting to get to know them better. She had a habit of watching people for a few moments, trying to size them up before uttering so much as a word. He wondered if she was simply letting him run this show or if Mary's knowledge of what was happening to the Blackstocks had frightened her.

Mary led them into her house by taking them up a long flight of sun-faded wooden stairs that connected her back porch directly to the beach. A single tiny dune and a ragged portion of fence was all that separated the stairs from the harder packed sand of the beach below.

"You know how most beach houses have those cutesy names like Seagull Landing or Beach Bum or what have you?" Mary asked.

"Yeah."

"Well this is Piper's Rest," she said. "I don't know how familiar you are with the pirate folklore around here, but Piper was this vagabond pirate that has some pretty great stories tied to him."

"You hear that?" Stephanie said, finally speaking up and playfully nudging Cooper. "Pirates!"

"Quiet, you," he hissed.

Mary smiled at them and Cooper saw her quickly glance to his left hand, probably looking for a ring.

Cute, he thought. *She's checking to see if Steph and I are married.*

Mary led them inside her house where Cooper saw a very well-maintained space. Most everything was laid out very similar to the Blackstock residence. The back sliding glass door opened onto a large living area with a connected kitchen. Two hallways led in opposite directions. The hall in front of them led to a large open staircase that boasted a landing adorned with a picture window.

Several boxes and two suitcases were pushed against the

wall. Cooper assumed these were the last remnants of Mary's upcoming move to Massachusetts.

"So what do you have to show me?" Cooper asked.

"A few things, actually," Mary said as she walked into the kitchen and opened up a drawer. She removed a small book that looked like a diary of sorts, complete with a pen sticking out of the top, resting in the spine.

"This is the first thing," she said, handing the book over to Cooper.

He opened it and flipped through the pages. There were numerous handwritten entries. From the looks of the handwriting, the entries had been written by several different people. Just as he began to understand what he was seeing, Mary started to explain.

"Most beach house owners leave out a book to let the renters leave little comments about how they enjoyed their time in their homes. In mine, you'll see that I've had people from all over the country stay here at Piper's Rest. I even had a family from Poland stay here a few summers back. But what I think might interest you," she said, reaching over and rifling through the pages as Cooper held the book open, "are notes like this one."

She pointed to a note that was written in thin print. It was dated July 5th, 2018. Cooper felt Stephanie sidling up next to him so she could also read it.

The note read:

LOVELY HOUSE. *We really liked the fact that the beach in this area isn't crowded. Have to say though…we think Piper's Rest might have some ghosts! LOL! Doors opened and closed by themselves and, on two occasions, we heard a kid talking late at night. We had a great time at your house but are leaving a bit freaked out. All the best!*

• • •

THE NOTE WAS SIGNED *the Abraham family – Abilene, TX.* Cooper read the note again and started flipping through the pages.

"There's another one here," Mary said. "This is the longest one. There are about a dozen or so others like this, out of roughly fifty entries."

Again, Cooper read an entry from the guest book, looking over the handwriting of someone he had never met but felt somehow connected to. It was another of those odd feelings he'd been having ever since his return.

He read it, holding it close to him so that Stephanie could easily see it, too.

WE CAME to the beach for some fun and relaxation. We got plenty of that, but we also got something else. We got a firm belief in the afterlife! On four occasions, we saw objects move of their own accord: the TV remote, a glass, the picture of the dunes on the wall on the 1st floor, and one of my husband's sandals. Our laptop also kept cutting on and off without us being anywhere near it. Last night, our fifteen year old son woke up and swore that there was someone else in his room with him. You have a very pretty home and the beach is peaceful and beautiful here, but please understand that I could not recommend your home to someone wanting to have a restful vacation.

We're leaving in an hour or so and my son is eerily quiet. I have considered calling the emergency contact # you left with us but don't want to make this any more real than it already is. I will leave it all in this note and hopefully leave all of this behind us.

THE NOTE WAS DATED August 17th, 2021 and was signed by Liz Follen of Richmond, Virginia.

"Did you know the house had this activity before you started renting it out?" Cooper asked.

"Yes. I've known since 2008 or so. But none of the renters ever said anything about it. It wasn't until about five or six years

ago that the renters started getting vocal about it. I always just
assumed that the ghosts, or whatever they were, went dormant
when new people showed up."

Stephanie reached for the book and Cooper handed it to her
as he started to look around the room. She had a look of caution
about her, like she expected someone to jump out from behind
the kitchen bar or from around the corner to the hallway.

"Have you ever felt in danger?" Cooper asked.

"Not really. I'm pretty sure the ghosts are children. That's
very sad, of course, but I can sense a sort of playfulness in whatever is going on here."

"Children? You're sure?"

"I've heard children laughing, yes. And some of the things
they do is like what a child seeking attention would do. One
morning, just a few months ago, I couldn't find my car keys. I
looked everywhere for them and ended up finding them in the
fridge."

"Considering the fact that the Blackstocks lost a child,"
Cooper said, "you can see why I would want you to be *certain*
that you're talking about kids, right?"

"Yes."

"So you're sure?"

She smiled. "Yes, I am positive."

"How?"

"Because I've figured out a way to communicate with them."

The answer surprised him, especially when he saw the
amused smile on Mary's face.

"That can be very dangerous if you don't know what you're
doing," Cooper warned.

"So I've read. But I think I've come up with something that's
pretty safe."

With that, she walked to one of the packed boxes against the
far living room wall. She dug around inside of it for a bit and
pulled out an old battered Scrabble game. She opened the box

and pulled out the velvet sack that held the letters. She shook it, letting Cooper hear the tiles clinking together inside.

"Scrabble tiles," he said. "That actually works?"

"Oh yes. They seem to enjoy it."

"Have you *seen* any entities?"

"No," Mary answered. "Sometimes I think I see something out of the corner of my eye, but it turns out to be nothing. Either that or they disappear before I can set my eyes on them."

Cooper took the bag of Scrabble tiles and put his hand inside, feeling the letters. He grinned, disappointed that he had never thought of such an exercise when he had been deeply involved in researching the paranormal. At its core, it was a simple idea but he supposed, based on all he knew of poltergeist activity, that it could work.

"Hey, Cooper?" Stephanie said.

He turned to see that Stephanie had sat down in the recliner at the edge of the living room. She held the book out to him and when he took it from her, he saw that she looked terrified.

"Read this one," she said, pointing to an entry at the top of a page. Cooper took it and started reading. The entry was dated July 2nd, 2019.

GREAT WEEK, great house, and beautiful beach. We really enjoyed having coffee on the patio while watching the sun come up over the beach every morning. But we're leaving this note to say that we think your house might be haunted. We've seen a few other entries in this book that hint at this, too. There was nothing too bad about the things we experienced—they were actually sort of cool. The creepiest thing we encountered was waking up at 3:00 in the morning to a boy's voice right outside of the bedroom door, whispering "dark water" over and over again.

FOURTEEN

ive minutes later, Cooper and Stephanie were sitting on
Mary Guthrie's back porch. Mary remained inside to give
them their privacy. After reading the entry, Cooper had handed
the guestbook back to Stephanie. But rather than take the book
back, Stephanie got up from the recliner without a word and
headed out onto the back porch. Cooper had excused himself
and followed her out, still holding the bag of Scrabble tiles.

Sitting across from one another at Mary's patio table,
Stephanie seemed to be in serious thought about something. She
had pulled her sunglasses down over her eyes when she stepped
out, so Cooper wasn't able to read anything in her eyes. Her
rigid posture and absolute silence made him think that she was
reaching the point that most skeptics often hit head-on when
suddenly confronted with undeniable proof of the paranormal.

For some reason, the sight on the rocks last night hadn't quite
done it. But now she was facing it in the form of reinforcement
from the guestbook and wasn't sure how to handle it. That was
Cooper's guess anyway.

"Talk to me," he said, wanting badly to put an arm around
her but knowing that she would pull away.

"I'd love to," she said, "but I don't know what to say."

"Take your time, then. Think it out."

She did. They sat two feet apart from one another, the tiled tabletop catching slight glimmers of the morning sun. Waves crashed behind them and the gnat-like noise of an airplane flying over the ocean, carrying a tacky advertising banner, crept in. Cooper watched the course of the plane as he waited for Stephanie to collect her thoughts. As he watched the plane, he craned his neck to the left and saw the two black rocks in the distance. They jutted up from the ocean like ghastly sentinels. From this distance, they looked small and insignificant. But the memory of last night was far too fresh in his mind to accept that illusion. No matter how small they seemed in the distance, they loomed large in his mind.

"I wish I could help," Stephanie finally said after several minutes. "I really do. But even if I knew where to start, I don't *want* to help. This is too much for me, Cooper. I can't just openly accept these things...things I didn't believe twelve hours ago and now....well, now I don't know. Or maybe I do know and just don't want to accept it. Do you understand that?"

"Yes, I think do," he said. And although he had always bought into the paranormal, he genuinely did understand what she was dealing with. He'd seen it countless times in his course of work, back when he'd had a normal life...or as normal as the life of a paranormal investigator could be.

"So I think I'm going to go for now," she said. "I was leaving this afternoon anyway. I'm just getting a five-hour head start."

"Stephanie, I can try to help y—"

"I know you can," she interrupted. "And I know you'd love to. But I'm not ready for it. Not for the ghost stuff and, honestly, not for you. It hurts to be with you, Cooper. It really does. That girl that came running to your hotel last night because she was scared...that's not me. That's never been me and you know it."

This was an overstatement, but Cooper wasn't about to say as much. He was too busy dealing with the fact that she was leaving. He knew she'd be gone later that afternoon, but he felt as if he was being robbed of four or five hours' worth of time with her. That, coupled with everything else they had experienced together in the last nine hours or so, made it even harder.

And that was exactly why he understood her need to leave.

"I understand," he said. "But what are you going to do? Are you just going to go back to work? Just like that?"

"I have to. I have to find normalcy after all of this. I have to bore myself."

"When can I see you again?"

She grinned at him and took her sunglasses off. He saw the fear in her eyes and wished she had left the glasses on. He couldn't remember wanting to embrace someone so badly in all of his life.

She looked at him as sincerely as she was able, leaned across the table, and gave him a soft and brief kiss on the mouth.

"You be safe here and do what you need to do," she said. "When you're done, email me. Don't call. Give me the option of returning the email. If I'm up to it, I'll reply and we'll figure this out. But for right now, all of this is just too much."

Cooper's heart felt like it was twisting in his chest but he managed to say, "Okay," without his voice breaking.

Stephanie stood up and opened her arms to him. He went to her and wrapped his own around her. It brought back the flood of memories from the year or so they had been together and made him wonder if they would have lasted if he hadn't so foolishly jumped headfirst into his own interests. Thinking of his now-mythic book while holding her made him angry with himself.

"Don't disappear on me again," she said into his ear. He was pretty sure she was fighting back tears.

"I won't. As long as you're going to be around."

She made a soft laughing sound against his neck and then, with a final squeeze, she let him go and started down Mary Guthrie's porch stairs.

Cooper watched her go. She walked in the opposite direction

of the way they had come, headed for the little sandy thorough-fares that wound between the houses. Cooper realized that she was his ride back to the motel but figured that, if it came down to it, he could walk the two miles.

Watching her leave, her hair blowing in the late morning breeze, he was aware that she was the only person alive that knew his secret. While there were two people that knew he had returned and was no longer missing (the other being the former co-worker that had set him up with a residence and bank accounts under the radar), Stephanie was the only one that knew the mission he had set himself upon. She was the only other one that knew how he had his financial matters set up.

With one single phone call or email, she could blow his cover and get him in some very big trouble.

But he knew that she wouldn't do such a thing. Besides, he was more worried about *her* disappearing on *him* this time. Why would she want to keep up with him, tying herself to his madness in the process? She didn't deserve it and the only reason she'd be willingly linked to it was because of him.

Cooper stood against the porch rail and watched her go until she angled up towards the other beach houses and headed down a stretch of unmarked blacktop. From there, she disappeared behind a tall fence on her way back to her car.

Then, just like the ghosts and specters Cooper had spent so much of his life chasing, she was there one moment and gone the next.

FIFTEEN

"**I**s everything okay?" Mary asked as Cooper came back in through the sliding glass door.

"Yeah," Cooper said, but without much effort to sound convincing.

"I'm sorry. I didn't mean to cause any trouble."

"You didn't. This would have happened eventually anyway. But, at the risk of sounding rude, that's not why I came back inside to speak with you."

"Of course. I'm sorry."

"It's okay," he said, picking the guest book back up. "I just need to piece this all together. You see, there's an entry in here where someone says they heard a young boy's voice saying the words *dark water* over and over. It just so happens that those were the last words that Henry Blackstock ever spoke before he drowned."

"Oh my God." The words came out in a whisper and, in a moment, Mary's face seemed to go pale. She suddenly looked to be three shades lighter than when she had first introduced herself on the beach half an hour ago.

"Now, I'm not going to make the leap and say that Henry

Blackstock's ghost is haunting your house," Cooper said, "but it does seem odd."

"Wouldn't he prefer to see his own family?" she asked. "Why choose my house to roam around in the afterlife?"

Cooper didn't know if it was the result of Stephanie's sudden decision to leave or not, but he found Mary's flippant attitude towards the topic aggravating. He tried to hide it, though, doing his best to stay focused.

"I don't know," he answered. "But I actually think there's more to this than you might assume. And I can't jump to any conclusions."

"What do you mean *more to this*? What else should I know?"

"Nothing for now." He already didn't like the fact that he had divulged information about Henry Blackstock to this woman. He certainly didn't see how telling her about Henry pointing towards the black rocks prior to his death would benefit her. And as for the ghoulish figure he and Stephanie had seen last night, there was absolutely no reason to share that information with her, either.

"Is there anything I can do to help you get answers for the Blackstocks?" Mary asked. "That's what they want, right? Answers? They called those ghost hunting people to their home. It was all over the rumor mill around this end of the beach."

"Yes, they need answers. But first, what can you tell me about Sam and Jenny Blackstock? Do you know them well?"

"We're certainly not close friends or anything," Mary said. "We wave when we pass one another. They're considered the odd ducks on this stretch of beach because they're the only ones that don't routinely rent their house out for the summer."

"Did you know them at all when their son died?"

"Yes. That was also the year I lost my husband."

"I'm sorry for your loss."

"It is what it is," she said, her flippant attitude once again coming to the surface. "He died in a car accident in November of that same year. But he actually helped out with the searches for

Henry when they were still taking place. I assume you know that his body was never found?"

"Yes."

"Sam and Jenny mostly stayed to themselves after all of that. I haven't had a meaningful conversation with either of them in several months."

"That's fine," Cooper said. "What I'm more interested in are these."

He handed her back the bag of Scrabble tiles, which she took like a greedy child. Mary reached into the bag and plucked one out, as if for dramatic effect. She held up an E tile and looked at it.

"Two years ago, I had a gentleman over," she said. "It was odd, as it was the first man I had spent any significant time with since my husband died. We had some wine and played Scrabble. It was my way of letting him know that I wasn't ready for anything intimate, you know? Anyway, the night went on and he left. I was tired, slightly buzzed, and feeling depressed. I went straight to bed, leaving the wine glasses and the Scrabble board on the kitchen table. I woke up the next morning to a simple message on my kitchen table, written out in Scrabble letters. There were six tiles. Two words, one on top of the other. It said *Hi Mary*. If I'm being honest, it freaked me out."

"How do you know it wasn't something left over from when your visitor left?"

"I thought the same thing when I saw the tiles. I was so sure he'd left the message that I thought nothing of it at first. I picked the tiles up and put them in the bag. I went to the coffee maker and when I turned my back, the letters were all spilled on the floor. I had set the bag on the board, near the center of the table. But somehow, they all spilled on the floor. I turned around and actually saw the tiles scattering around on the floor, like invisible hands were sorting through them. I watched the tiles get sorted, and several tiles got separated from the rest. This time, the message was *Good Morning*."

A familiar thrill started to worm its way through Cooper—the feeling of something truly bizarre just around the corner. It never got old, no matter how small the story, and Mary Guthrie's was shaping up to be something special.

"That was it?" he asked.

"That time, yes. Of course, once I realized there was something very odd going on in my home, I had to try it out a few more times. It was scary but my curiosity wouldn't let it go, you know? That morning, I was too frightened. I left the house and didn't come back until later that night. It took time, courage and a few bottles of wine before I could give it a real try."

"Does it work every single time you do it?"

"No, not every time. It seems that the old clichés are true. The ghosts—or whatever they are—seem to really only want to participate at night. I'll sometimes get them to play early in the morning, but not often."

"What do you talk about?"

"Well, it's really like a game to them. And you see, I think that whatever ghosts are visiting my house...well, I don't think any of them are Henry Blackstock. I've asked for a name before and the only one I've gotten out of them is Amy."

"Amy," Cooper said. "Spelled out in Scrabble tiles?"

"Yes."

"What else have you asked?"

"I've asked how long she's been here and she said she didn't know. *Not sure,* is actually what she spelled. I asked her how old she was and she said twelve."

"Have you asked her if she knows she's dead?"

Mary shook her head. "It may seem silly, but I thought it might be rude."

Cooper didn't think it was silly at all. He knew from experience that there was a very strange sort of poise and set of manners that needed to be observed when communicating with the dead.

"Is there anything else you've asked and gotten a response to?" he asked.

"It's mostly small things. I've asked her what her favorite color is—it's green—and the names of her parents. But the one thing I asked her that she did answer that has always struck me as a little creepy was if she was happy here."

"What did she say?"

"She spelled out *Sometimes*. And then she mixed up the letters again and spelled *scared*. And then when I asked her what she was scared of, she said *the dark place*."

Cooper thought about this for a while, his eyes glancing back in the direction of Mary's sliding glass window and the beach beyond. He knew what he wanted to ask next. He wasn't afraid to ask it, but he knew there would be a strange and very involved path at the end of the question.

"Would you be willing to allow me to try it out tonight?" he asked.

"Of course," Mary said. "That is, if Amy doesn't mind. I've had company over several times since it started happening and she doesn't seem to want to show herself when new people are here. Even when I leave the Scrabble tiles out for her and go into another room with my company, she stays quiet. Again, I thought it might seem rude to her—like I was trying to train a pet or something."

Sometimes, such an excuse instantly convinced Cooper that the other person was full of crap—that all of their excuses were a sot-so-clever way to hide their obvious lie. But he'd seen liars and genuine souls alike, and they were often easy to tell apart. And based on everything his gut told him, Mary Guthrie was not telling lies.

"Don't worry," Cooper said with a nervous grin. "If there's a ghost here, I think they'll warm up to me. I sort of have a knack for these things."

HE LEFT Mary Guthrie's house and walked along the beach until he could see the back of the Blackstocks's house. He had planned on just walking by, hoping to be led or inspired or...or whatever. While he wouldn't come out and admit to himself that he was hoping for another of those psychic-like flashes, that was really what it boiled down to.

But when he saw the Blackstocks's back porch, he spotted Sam sitting at their patio table. He was sipping on a cup of coffee and looking out to the sea. When he saw Cooper approaching, he gave an unenthusiastic wave and motioned for him to come up.

Cooper walked up the sand, across the back yard, and onto the patio. He saw that Sam looked tired, his eyes glassy and his mouth drawn tight.

"Everything okay?" Cooper asked.

Sam shrugged. "Jenny's having a bad migraine this morning. I called into work and got permission to telecommute so I could stay here with her. I'll start soon, I guess."

"Does she get migraines often?"

"Not too often, but when they *do* hit, they can be terrible. She gets them during times of high stress. She had one for an entire week after Henry died. It started right after the service we had for him. I'm talking laid out in bed with the blinds drawn. I even had to tack up blankets over the closed blinds to keep light out. Thankfully, none since then have been that bad."

"Do you think my visit yesterday caused this one?"

"I won't lie...it probably contributed to it," Sam admitted. "Hearing kids laughing in our house in the middle of the night isn't helping either."

"Did you hear it again last night?"

"No, but I woke up around two or three in the morning and swore I heard footsteps."

"I just want to make sure," Cooper said. "If I'm infringing on your lives in any way, I'll stop."

"For now, we're okay with you looking into it. You seem sort of real, you know? Those ghost hunter guys were very rigid and somber. They seemed pissed that they didn't get any evidence and were a little too into themselves. As long as you don't get intrusive with us, we're okay. If I'm being honest, you sort of creep me out...you know...the visions or whatever. But it's proof that you're the real deal, I guess."

"I don't know about that."

They were silent for a moment as Sam sipped on his coffee and continued to stare out at the ocean.

"I met one of your neighbors this morning," Cooper said. "Mary Guthrie. How well do you know her?"

"Pretty well, I guess. She seems nice. Her husband died a while back and she sort of disappeared from all the social circles around here. She's hardly ever in her house because she rents it out all summer. How'd you end up meeting her?"

"I was checking out the area of beach where you guys were playing with Henry the day he died."

"Find anything?"

"No," Cooper lied. He wasn't about to tell him about the figure he had come face to face with last night. He still had no idea what that figure represented and wasn't absolutely positive it had anything to do with Henry. There was no use in upsetting him for what might potentially be nothing.

"So what else is on your agenda for the day?" Sam asked.

"I'm not sure. I'm sort of just winging this thing for right now. And as embarrassing as it might sound, I was wondering if I could maybe ask you a favor."

"Sure."

"I sort of got stranded without a car this morning. Do you think you could give me a ride back to my motel?"

"Sure thing," Sam said. "Just let me slip in and tell Jenny. You can cut around the yard and just meet me out front if you want. I'd invite you through the house, but Jenny is on the couch, laid up and trying to sleep her migraine off."

"Thanks. Let her know I hope she feels better."

Sam went inside, leaving Cooper on the patio. As he walked down the stairs, Cooper looked out to the ocean, trying to see it in the same light as Sam. It was vast, endless and, on a day as clear as this one, majestic and beautiful. Gulls cried out and boats zipped across the water. A bit further down, a few families were sitting out on the sand. Just another day at the beach.

But to the Blackstocks, Cooper assumed it must look different. To them, it was nothing more than one large and endless tomb that their son would remain inside forever.

SIXTEEN

I t was hard for Cooper to imagine that the main stretch of road connecting all of the side streets and businesses would be packed in a few weeks. The traffic puttering along it, as Sam carried him to the motel, seemed casual at best. No one was in a hurry and there was plenty of space between every car. The beauty of the unblemished late spring morning was pristine, even with the beach hidden by shops and motels. He wondered if it felt like this all of the time before all of the tourists came in.

"You know," Sam said, breaking Cooper's concentration. "I went ahead and Googled you. I couldn't resist."

"And you still chose to give me a ride?" He forced a laugh behind the comment but felt that it might have been a little leading.

"Nothing I read made me think any less of you. But it did make me wonder, though."

"About what?"

"I don't want to pry," Sam said. "Honestly, there are things I'd be scared to know, I think."

"Well, ask me anything. I'll be as honest as I can."

Sam took a moment to give something a lot of thought, then finally gave in to his curiosity. "As far as the FBI, and all of the agencies that were looking for you, are concerned, you're still missing. The general consensus is that you're dead. Is that right?"

"That's right."

"So why risk going so public? When you introduced yourself to me and Jenny, you didn't even bother with a fake name."

It was a good question, and something that Cooper had thought long and hard about after he had made all of his arrangements prior to driving out to North Carolina to start on his journey. He had nearly decided to use a fake name but, in the end, had decided against it.

"It's really a matter of honesty," Cooper said. "In the case of you and Jenny, I tried to imagine what parents that had lost a child would think of a man that gave them a fake name. Really, if I *had* given a fake name, you could have probably done some digging on the internet and found out who I was pretty easily, right?"

"Yeah."

"So then why take the risk of ruining what is already a very shaky sort of trust with complete strangers?" Cooper asked. "It simply wasn't worth the risk."

"Well, what happens if someone decides to turn you in? What's stopping me from giving the FBI a call and saying that, not only is Cooper Reid alive and well, but investigating the death of my son and the haunting of my house?"

"Nothing would be stopping you," Cooper said. "Nothing at all. But I should tell you that I certainly hope you don't plan to do that."

Sam smiled and shook his head. "No. I'm not going to do that."

"Thanks."

"Just so you know, there's quite a bit of information online that makes you sound like a rock star. I found a YouTube clip of you on FOX News talking about how the FBI and CIA don't take the supernatural seriously. You were on there with one of those UFO nuts."

"I met a lot of UFO nuts in my time," Cooper said. "The really scary thing is that most of them were on to something."

"Did you ever find any solid evidence of UFOs?"

"Solid as in presentable as evidence to the scientific community? No. Enough to convince me? Absolutely."

"What about ghosts?"

"I found more than enough to back up my own beliefs, but nothing that science would ever verify."

"So...if you don't mind me asking, where were you for the time you were missing?"

Cooper briefly thought of the conversation he'd shared with Stephanie the night before about this very topic. His inability to answer it was maddening, especially when being quizzed so innocently by a man that was hopefully starting to trust him.

"I'm not sure," Cooper answered.

"For real?"

"For real."

Whether it was the stern look on Cooper's face or the sense of impending awkwardness within the car, Sam left it at that. Cooper took advantage of the break in conversation to do some digging of his own. There was no subtle way to transition the conversation, so he simply asked the question that was on his mind.

"I don't suppose there are any cave systems around here anywhere, are there?"

Sam thought about it for a moment and then shrugged. "Not that I know of. Not anymore, at least."

"What do you mean?"

"Well, I don't know the history behind it, but I think there was some sort of cavern attraction at one of the campgrounds outside of town at one time. I'm pretty sure it's gone belly-up, though. One of those tacky tourist traps that only last a season or two, you know?"

"Do you know what kind of attraction it was?" Cooper asked.

"Not really. I think it was something for the history buffs. It was about pirates landing here and hiding away from their enemies. Treasure hunts and swashbuckling and all of that."

"Interesting."

"Not really. If you live around here long enough, the pirate crap gets boring. Every restaurant, every putt-putt golf course. Even those stupid decals on the back of tourist's cars."

Cooper laughed, having seen his share of those decals since he had arrived in Kill Devil Hills two days ago.

They remained silent as Sam turned off of the highway and into the lot of Cooper's motel. Cooper felt like he and Sam could talk a while longer if they wanted, even if it was nothing more than exchanging thoughts on the weather. Sam seemed like a relatable guy—something Cooper had not noticed yesterday.

"Thanks for the ride. Let Jenny know that I hope her headache gets better soon."

"It will. These things come and go. She'll be better by tonight."

"I hope so. But tell me honestly…do you think her headaches have anything to do with the activity in your house?"

"I don't know," Sam said with a heavy sigh. "I've wondered about that myself."

"Well, look…I'm in room twenty-eight. If there's anything I can do, don't hesitate to call."

"I'll do that."

With that, Cooper stepped out of the car. He gave a wave of appreciation and watched Sam Blackstock pull back out onto the highway before walking to his room. On his way, he pulled his cell phone out of this pocket, hoping that he had maybe missed a text or call from Stephanie.

But there was nothing.

He pocketed the phone and entered his room. Knowing that Stephanie had been here this morning and was now simply gone made him feel profoundly lonely. It was a feeling he had grown accustomed to over the years, specifically after leaving the FBI and the shadow organization that had recruited him, but it never truly got easy to handle.

He closed the door behind him and, as was his norm, closed himself off to everything outside so that he could think about the parts of the world so often shrouded in shadows.

SEVENTEEN

W ith the rest of the day at his disposal, Cooper found himself with nothing to do. The fact that he was at the beach made it very hard for him to stay in his motel room, so he ended up taking his laptop to a small pier-side bar where he enjoyed two-dollar beer specials and a bottomless shrimp plate for five bucks. All in all, not a bad lunch.

The bar was fairly crowded, considering that it was only 1:30, so Cooper chose an umbrella-covered patio table along the edge of the pier. He connected to the bar's WiFi and did a little more research. This time, however, he wasn't interested in pirates and caves. What Sam had told him gave him a bit more to go on, but Cooper wasn't quite certain that was the route he needed to take.

Not yet, anyway.

It was amazing how rusty his research skills had become in the time that had passed since he had been steadily at work on his second book. Now, knowing that there was no paycheck and a great degree of uncertainty about his future, he found research tedious and boring no matter what the subject matter was. He figured that if Stephanie had still been there, she'd likely be a huge help with the research end of things.

Thinking of her, he pulled out his pay-as-you-go cellphone

and dialed her number. It rang four times and then went to voicemail. He considered leaving a message but hung up before the beep.

Disappointed, he turned back to his laptop and started trying to uncover a path of research that might shed some light on why the area of beach containing Mary Guthrie's house and the two black rocks might be haunted. He did a random search on deaths in the area but found very little at first. As he had expected, the bulk of deaths in the area came during the summer. A few were the result of car accidents as tourists started filling up the roads. But there were also a few drowning deaths, most of which were surprisingly not very close to shore but further out. He found stories about people having scuba diving accidents, falling off party boats, and even a rather grisly fishing accident. But there were not many reports of people drowning near the shore.

Still, there were enough to sift through. By the time he was on his second beer, he had found something of a groove. It was nowhere near the trance-like states he'd often enjoyed in the handful of years before his disappearance, but it made him remember what it was like.

He had very little trouble finding stories on Henry Blackstock. The stories he read all verified what the Blackstocks had told him: Henry had been there one moment and gone the next, as if the tide had sucked him down with spiteful intent. While there was no hard proof, it had been assumed that Henry had fallen in shallow water and was then pulled out by the undertow. His body had never been recovered.

Cooper knew that he was limited with just the internet at his disposal and figured he might have more luck at the local library. But he quite honestly didn't feel like going through all of that. He kept having to remind himself that he was no longer the Cooper M. Reid that pieced books together, using lurid facts and morbid histories to weave his narratives together. No...the research he was doing now was for something much more substantial. In this case, he hoped he could help the Blackstocks get some sort of closure in regards to their son and the paranormal events occurring in their home.

Even without a library's deeper resources at hand, Cooper discovered five other drowning deaths that had occurred in the last seven years. In addition to those, there were three other stories about close calls where someone had been pulled out to sea and rescued by a lifeguard or fast-thinking family member. He figured that there were many more instances of this occurring that simply hadn't made the headlines. While none of the articles on the drownings gave a specific location, one of them did describe the area as being *"on a stretch of beach beyond several rental properties, bordered by a rocky hillside on the west end of Kill Devil Hills."*

As far as Cooper was concerned, that was pretty accurate to the same location he had been checking out—the same place where Henry Blackstock has been sucked out to sea.

And the same location where he had seen that grisly apparition.

He snapped the top of his computer down and looked out to the ocean. He started to get his thoughts into order, sorting through what was important and what was probably not. The connections were there. And Sam Blackstock mentioning campgrounds had him thinking about another approach...something linked to the stories of pirates he'd been reading about.

There was coincidence, and then there was eerie certainty.

Never one to jump to conclusions of any kind, Cooper was beginning to feel the latter in terms of what was happening on the beach beside Mary Guthrie's house.

He considered grabbing another beer but thought that it might be best to remain as clear-headed as possible for the remainder of the day. It was only 2:30, and he still wanted to drive out to the campgrounds to see if there was anything to Sam's story about the old caverns.

Cooper paid his tab and headed back down the pier with his laptop bag over his shoulder. As he made his way to his car, he began to feel a creeping sort of certainty coming over him. He had felt it several times before when he was on the brink of discovery. It was almost like a sixth sense, similar to hearing a phone ring and being absolutely certain that there was bad news on the other end. It was a sensation he'd once tried to explain in a *Newsweek* interview when he had been at the height of his popularity—about a year before his disappearance.

He'd used the phone metaphor in that interview but as he climbed behind the wheel of his car, he didn't think that description did it justice this time. Now, he thought it was more like feeling someone lightly tapping him on the shoulder and turning around to find that there's no one there at all.

But the tapping continues.

In this case, it seemed that the source of the tapping was simply waiting to be discovered before it was going to let him see it.

Cooper pulled out into traffic and started formulating a plan as to how he might find that particular source.

EIGHTEEN

I t took a bit of driving, but Cooper managed to find the locations of the only two active campgrounds in the area. One was located off the beaten path, on the other side of the highway from the countless beach businesses and sandy shores. The entrance to it was nearly hidden in the scraggly undergrowth of forest that sat on the opposite side of the road from the beach.

He quickly learned that this campground was likely not the one he was looking for. It was primarily nothing more than hiking trails, a small pond, a battered playground in desperate need of an update, and a few bare patches of ground that were branded with the burn marks of campfires past. The grounds were overgrown and badly cared for. Cooper wasn't at all surprised to see that there were only two campers and a single van using the grounds.

He wasted no time at this location, sensing from the layout and neglect alone that it had probably never boasted anything that might even remotely resemble a tourist attraction—even if that attraction was really nothing more than a big hole in the ground.

Twenty minutes after leaving, he passed a billboard on the

side of the road that informed him of the second campground. The board was simple and rustic, made of wood and faded paint. It read: SADDLEBACK CAMPGROUNDS. CAMPING, FISHING, SPORTS, FUN! 6 MILES AHEAD.

Cooper drove toward the campgrounds, noting when he passed the side road that led to the Blackstock and Guthrie houses. He set his odometer to zero, wanting to clock the distance between the houses and the campgrounds. Unless the caverns Sam had mentioned were fairly close to the houses and the black rocks, he didn't see how the two could be connected. But if he had learned one thing during his time researching the paranormal—and even before that, in his more formal time with the FBI—it was to not make assumptions about anything. This was especially true when the target you were after was abstract.

And if the thing he had seen on those rocks last night wasn't *abstract*, he didn't know what was.

When he reached Saddleback Campgrounds, he found that the entrance, like the first campground he had visited, was on the side of the road opposite the beach. When he turned in, his odometer read 4.6; there was just over four and a half miles between Saddleback and the black rocks.

Right away, Cooper could tell that this campground was much better maintained than the first one. The grass was trimmed meticulously along the entrance road, the sides of which were bordered with elegant pieces of what looked to be driftwood, set into lackadaisical patterns. The entrance road was less than a quarter of a mile long and came to an end at a fork in the road. To the right, there was a small white building that served as the visitor station. To the left, another road began. Wooden arrows told him that campgrounds, playgrounds, and fishing were located down this road.

He toyed with the idea of stopping by the visitor's center but thought it might be best to get a basic lay of the land for himself. Besides, he didn't feel like listening to an over-enthusiastic guide tell him how great the campgrounds were.

Cooper took the road to the left, passing more beautifully manicured grass. Patches of beach sand were sporadically placed within the lawn, one of which had a volleyball net strung up. Roughly one hundred yards down the road, trees and thick vegetation suddenly took over and Cooper felt like he had been transported to some picturesque lane in the country. Within just a few yards of this transition, he watched a crane take flight from a nearby tree.

A few thin unpaved roads began to appear on the sides of the road. Rustic wooden markers with embossed white letters pointed down each one, boasting various activities: camping, fishing, kayaking, disc golf, and hiking. Sam had told him that the cavern attraction had shut down years ago, so Cooper wasn't expecting to see a sign for it. Still, he kept an eye out, wondering if maybe a sign had been left up for the sake of nostalgia.

He narrowed his choices down, assuming that caves and caverns wouldn't be located directly near areas where fishing and kayaking were in high demand. And he didn't think any state park in their right mind would place open campgrounds near a known cave system. That led Cooper to believe that if there had once been a cavern-type attraction on the grounds, it had probably been somewhere along the hiking trails.

He stopped his car, turning around at the mouth of the road that led down to one of several disc golf courses. He drove back toward the road that led to the hiking trails, a little irritated with himself for not stopping by the visitor's center for a map of the place first.

Cooper came to the road in question and turned down it, glad to see that it was smooth and mostly flat despite not being paved. Within a few feet, he saw a car pulled to the side of the trail with one of those pretentious runner decals on the back glass, letting the world know the distance of the marathon they had run.

Ahead, he saw a small marker sticking up from the ground that read **Echo Trail: 3.5 MILES.** A thin footpath began beside it, faintly etched out in the ground. Several yards past that, on the other side of the road, another marker read **Hubbard Trail: 1.7 MILES**. As he made his way down the dirt road, he saw several other markers like this, stationed in front of trails that wound off into the forest. He passed two more vehicles along the road that had pulled over by these markers.

A little less than half a mile farther down, he came to another marker on the right side of the road. There was a larger one situated directly next to it. The sign was made of marble, standing perhaps three feet out of the ground. On it, two paragraphs had been written in bold black letters. He had seen several of these in his travels, particularly in areas within the South where the history of the Civil War was still highly revered.

Cooper stopped the car and got out. He walked up to the sign and read it.

PICKMAN'S TRAIL (1.4 miles)

Pickman's Trail is not necessarily beloved for the hike it offers. At less than a mile and a half long, the real treasure to be found rests at the end of the trail: Pickman's Caverns. Pickman's Caverns once attracted tourists and history lovers of all kinds. These historic caverns are where fabled thief, pirate, and murderer, Douglass Pickman hid away in 1759 when angry locals chased him down following his involvement in a robbery and the murder of at least seven locals during the heist.

The caverns were closed in 2012 due to safety hazards, but the legend of Douglass Pickman's bloody legacy lives on.

COOPER GRINNED NERVOUSLY at the sign and then, without a second thought, started down the thin trail that wound between the marker and the historical sign. He knew nothing about Douglass Pickman. He'd never even heard the name before today. He imagined that a tour guide bringing curious people to the caverns would have explained the history in better detail than the sign.

Cooper figured he could always look it up later.

For now, he had a hike to endure.

THERE WERE obvious signs of use along Pickman's Trail, but it was also evident that it had mostly gone forgotten over the last few years. Within fifty yards or so, Cooper spotted a granola bar wrapper, an old soda can, and a tattered plastic bag partially covered by the debris and dead foliage along the ground. Apparently, the grounds crew had forgotten about Pickman's Trail just as the tourists had.

It wasn't a very scenic trail, offering only scrubby trees, briars, and tall weeds that had started to creep up through the forest floor. The overhang of branches above his head from the few taller trees provided a slight shade, but not enough to keep him from sweating. The sheer number of cobwebs strung up across the trail from branch to branch was further proof that no one had been down the trail for a while. He walked on, wiping cobwebs from his face and hair. He listened to the natural sounds of the forest, struck by how it felt like a different world out here, totally removed from the beach.

After slightly more than twenty minutes, he came to the end of the trail. There was no scenic look-out or grand viewpoint that may have one day thrilled visitors; it simply stopped in the form of a dead end. Directly in front of him, there was a significant rise to the ground, where fragments of rock jutted out of the earth and pointed upwards, creating a leaning wall that stood about eight feet tall. It was perfectly cradled by softer earth to all sides except in the few areas where the slate-colored rock peeked through. It was cradled at the top by dirt, weeds, and over-hanging roots from the rest of the forest beyond.

Slightly to the left along the rock, several boards had been

bolted to the surface. There were eight two-by-fours, nailed to
what looked like several sheets of plywood. All of it had been
bolted into the rock, sitting slightly askew. The wood looked
secure but aged. A black metal sign had been applied to the
boards, reading DO NOT ENTER in large orange letters.

Some genius had used a black marker underneath the sign
and added: THAT'S WHAT SHE SAID.

Cooper walked up to the boards and checked the edges. It
was secured tightly, but he found that he could slide his fingers
behind a few warped areas along the back of the plywood base.
He got a grip on the right side of the makeshift wooden gate and
pulled as hard as he could. He braced his feet and pulled back
until his shoulders and back ached. The wood creaked and
moaned at the force, but the plywood was simply too strong and
the bolts were sturdy and strong. He was pretty sure that there
were at least three sheets of plywood stacked behind one
another.

He gave it another try, putting everything he had into it. This
time, the first sheet of plywood splintered and cracked along the
edge but it wasn't nearly enough to budge the wood.

Panting, Cooper looked at the boards and rolled his eyes. In
the past, when he'd been working for the government, a simple
call would have resulted in a team showing up with crowbars
and axes or anything else he'd need. With a sigh, he ran his
hands over the boards, pressing against them and looking for
any area that seemed weaker than the rest.

It all seemed pretty solid but, within a few seconds, none of
that mattered. He felt his head getting slightly swimmy, and the
boards felt like warm rubber beneath his hands.

He suddenly became aware that a vision was coming—just
like the one he had experienced involving Henry Blackstock
when he had rested his hands upon the Blackstocks's front door.

He tried to prepare himself for it but it came fast, sweeping
across his mind like sand blown across the plains by a hurricane.
It trundled through his head almost violently and he saw

—a tall tour guide taking a group of twenty or so through an opening in the side of the rock wall. The entrance to the cave is lit by two small lights installed in the floor. Beyond that, there is a very slight drop to the ground. The tour guide points these out and as the tourists file behind him, watching their step, a series of stairs and guardrails come into view. Small lights have also been installed along the stairways. The tour guide takes several steps down and, within a few yards, the cavern opens up, allowing more room. Ahead of him, there are more stairs; some of them are wooden and bolted into the rock. Others are made of metal. The stairs lead further down as the earth opens up wide beneath them—

This vision was not nearly as powerful as the one he'd had about Henry Blackstock. This one was fuzzy, wavering like summer heat from asphalt. But still, it had been unmistakable. He'd seen the tour guide in great detail, right down to his black mustache and the beginnings of gray at the corners of it. Someone in the tour group had been wearing a North Carolina Tarheels tank top. The man beside the Tarheel fan had sported a long tribal band tattoo on his left arm.

As far as Cooper was concerned, the vision was proof that Pickman's Caverns were behind this wooden blockade.

He also felt that it meant that he was supposed to get inside.

Cooper gave the blockade a final look, taking his hands slowly away from it. He supposed he could come back with a crowbar and an axe, and hope *that* might be enough to get through. Of course, if there was concrete reinforcement behind it, he was screwed. Again, it made him *almost* miss the conveniences of working for the government, even when working in the shadows.

Frustrated, Cooper turned back toward the trail and headed for his car. He followed the trail back to the road, starting to knit together a plan that he thought might lead him back into the darkness for the first time in nearly a year.

NINETEEN

With more than four hours remaining before he was due to meet Mary Guthrie at her house, Cooper decided it might be a good idea to stop by the campground's visitor center after all. If he planned to revisit Pickman's Trail with intentions of getting through the barricade, it would be helpful to know when the grounds had the least amount of security.

He also wondered if they might have some more information on Douglass Pickman.

He parked his car beside the only other car in the visitor center lot and stepped out. Standing in the parking lot and looking to the surrounding woodland, it was hard to believe that the beach was less than a mile to the east. The exterior decor of the visitor center was very beachy indeed. Palm trees jutted from the small lawn, and the parking lot was bordered with white sand and crushed seashells. It was quaint but it was all overly staged and cheap-looking.

He walked inside, finding a small but typical little visitor center. A counter ran along half of the front room, adorned with several spinning racks of brochures and coupon books. There was a man behind the counter, folding tee shirts with generic beach slogans on them: Salt Life, Salty Dog, Surrender Your

Booty, and unfortunate slogans of that nature. He looked up when Cooper walked in and gave a hearty smile.

"What can I do for you?" the man asked.

Cooper spotted the premier rack of brochures along the front of the counter and headed directly for them. "Nothing for now," he answered. "Just doing some snooping about local attractions and history."

"Well, just let me know if you need anything."

"Sure."

Cooper leafed through the pamphlets and brochures, passing recommendations for restaurants, family fun, and boat tours of the area. Every pamphlet looked exactly the same, promising fun and excitement. It wasn't until he reached the bottom row of advertisements that he found a brochure that mentioned Pickman's Cavern. It gave the same information the historical marker had given, with a footnote stating that the caverns had been closed since 2012 and the site was considered to be dangerous and off limits to the public.

Cooper slapped the brochure down on the counter. "What else do you have about this Pickman character?"

"Douglass Pickman?" the man behind the counter asked.

"Yeah."

"Not much. There are some really great stories about him that get passed around, but a lot of it is pretty grisly. The way I understand it, there were a lot of parents that would complain from time to time about the tour guides telling the stories when children were around."

"Are the stories historically accurate or just made up to sell stuff?"

"As far as I know, every story we ever told about him was true."

"Any idea why they closed Pickman's Caverns?"

"It wasn't safe," the employee said. "The further down you go into the caverns, it gets sort of treacherous. Even with the installed steps, it was pretty dangerous. A lot of people kept telling us that it was creepy down there, too. We thought about switching up the approach—maybe turning Pickman's Trail into a ghost walk sort of thing—but decided against it."

"Do you know the whole history of Pickman?"

"Just the bare bones, really. You interested in it?"

"Yeah. Just morbid curiosity, really."

"Well then, you want to talk to Jack Paulson. He used to do some of the tours through Pickman's Caverns. He's a local expert on just about anything you can think of. And he *loves* to talk about history."

"Does he work here?"

"He does. In fact, he's out back right now, fixing up one of our golf carts."

"You think he'd mind a visitor?" Cooper asked.

"Jack? No way. He'll talk your ear off if you let him."

"Thanks."

Cooper swiped up the brochure and exited the visitor's center. He walked around the side of the building, on a sidewalk bordered with sand and seashells. He carried the brochure in his hand and nervously started folding it. There was a bizarre feeling starting to stir in his gut—the sense that he had picked up a thread that was either going to lead him to some answers or cause something unseen to unravel.

When Cooper came around to the back of the shop, he saw a man bending over into the exposed battery compartment of a golf cart. The man was humming to himself as he worked. The volume at which he hummed indicated that he was not expecting visitors.

"Excuse me," Cooper said.

The man jerked a bit, clearly startled. When he looked up, there was an expression of slight irritation on his face. He was an older man, maybe pushing sixty or so. His tee shirt was matted in sweat and the OBX hat he wore was caked in oil and grime.

"Yeah?" the man asked.

"Are you Jack Paulson?"

"Yeah, that's me. And I don't mind saying that you just scared the daylights out of me." He chuckled then, the irritation gone. His smile was thin and his chuckle sounded raspy and broken, but genuine.

"Sorry," Cooper said.

"No worries. And yes, I'm Jack."

Cooper tried to say something else, but no words would come. He felt himself go cold and was momentarily paralyzed by a frozen sensation when he realized that he had seen Jack Paulson before.

Yeah, he thought. *I'm definitely on to something here.*

Jack was the tour guide Cooper had seen in his vision no more than half an hour ago.

He was currently smiling at Cooper uncertainly. It was like staring into the reflection of a vivid dream.

"You okay, son?" Jack asked. "You look like you just saw a ghost."

It was Cooper's turn to laugh nervously now. "Yeah. I get that a lot."

AFTER COOPER TOLD Jack Paulson what he was interested in, Jack led him to a small picnic table that sat in the shade to the right of the visitor's center. He took two Cokes out of a cooler that was sitting in the back of the golf cart and handed one to Cooper. They sat at the picnic table, drinking their sodas in the shade, as Jack started to talk.

Right away, Cooper could tell that the man in the visitor's center hadn't been exaggerating. Within two sentences, Jack had settled into story-teller mode. Cooper thought he might be the sort of man that, if he had grandchildren, would always find a kid on his lap, eager to hear a story. There was no real flair for the dramatic in the way he spoke, only the straight-shooting of a man that knew how to tell a good story.

"So why are you so interested in Douglass Pickman?" Jack asked.

Cooper felt an excuse that he had once used many times in his previous life coming to the tip of his tongue. He allowed it to escape and when he spoke it, he felt like someone had walked over his grave.

"I'm writing a book," he lied.

Jack seemed impressed as he leaned forward and gave a huge smile. "Well in that case, I'm more than happy to help."

"Thanks."

"Do you, by chance, know how Kill Devil Hills got its name?" Jack asked.

"No, I don't," Cooper said, although he had been struck by the morbid name on more than one occasion.

"Well, while there's no real concrete proof that I'm aware of, there are two stories. It doesn't matter which you believe, though. They both equate to the same thing. One story claims that locals woke up one morning in the late 1700s and found hundreds of barrels of rum washed up on the shore. There was other debris with the barrels, indicating that the rum had survived a shipwreck. Once they tried the rum, locals were fond of its ability to get them drunk pretty fast. They said the stuff was potent enough to kill the devil. Another story suggests that a pirate ship crashed somewhere very close to shore and the pirates that survived started brewing moonshine that also had the strength to kill the devil.

"The reason I tell you all of that is to get the pirate part of the story out of the way. I'm sure you've noticed that most businesses around here milk the pirate angle as much as they can. But it's legitimate. Around here—and along most of the coast and the sound, actually—the pirate culture really is a strong part of our history. It's one of the things we usually try to make visitors to the campground aware of."

"Was Douglass Pickman somehow associated with these stories?" Cooper asked.

"No, he came around a bit later. Some people claim that, when Douglass Pickman was a boy, he sailed with Blackbeard. He was well known for trying to take over Blackbeard's post and reputation several years or so after Blackbeard was killed."

"And you're talking about the *actual* Blackbeard that everyone knows about?"

"That's the one. His real name was Edward Teach. He was killed in 1718 when the crew of a competing ship overpowered him after he killed the captain."

Cooper found himself wishing that he *was* writing a book. History had always fascinated him and, if everything Jack Paulson was telling him was true, he had hit a gold mine of trivia. When he had gone rogue from the underbelly of the FBI—from a shadow organization that only a handful of people knew about—Cooper had carried a small recording device with him everywhere he went. He would have given anything in that moment to have that device on him so he could record Jack's story.

"But really, Pickman wasn't nearly as gruesome or as deadly as Edward Teach," Jack went on. "Many people think he *wanted* to be, but his story ends very differently than Teach or any other pirates of dubious reputations. That's why no one has ever really heard of him."

"So how did he come to end up in Kill Devil Hills?"

"Like any pirate did in those days: looking for goods to plunder, women to bed, and trouble to start. Pickman came to Kill Devil Hills in 1759. For the most part, the real threat of pirates was over by then. If you were going out to sea, there was some risk but it was pretty rare to see them coming ashore with any ill intent. When Pickman showed up, he had his ten year-old daughter with him. No one really knows anything about the mother. But if Pickman's life was like that of any other pirate of that time, it can be assumed that the mother either died, was captured by some other crew, or just up and left her family. And if her husband chose to live his life as a pirate, who could blame her?"

"So you mean to tell me that this so-called pirate was sailing the seas with a daughter in tow?"

"That's how the story goes," Jack said. "The real experts that document these kinds of things for historical records and whatnot have all but confirmed everything I'm telling you."

"That seems like a pretty harsh life for a child."

"I'm sure it was. But if a man like Pickman, that desired the pirate life, also wanted to keep his child, that says something as far as I'm concerned. Stand-up fathers were few and far between in Pickman's circles. Sadly, it's far too common today, too, if you want my opinion."

"So a pirate and a good father," Cooper remarked "Or, rather, as good as he could be."

"Yeah, that's what they say," Jack said. He took a gulp of his Coke and then started again. "Anyway, Pickman came ashore with a crew of about eight other men. From what we know, they legally purchased some rum, some clothes, and other goods. Some people even claim that Pickman's daughter played with some of the local kids along the beach while he did his business, but there's no proof of this.

"After their shopping, Pickman and his crew visited the bank. Back then, the banks were really just more like the town treasury. What we know for certain is that Pickman did not enter the bank. He stood outside with another crew member as a look-out. The men that went inside started shooting. When all was said and done, eight people within the treasury were killed and Pickman's crew left the building with around four thousand dollars...a nice sum in those days."

Cooper mulled all of this over while his bottle of Coke started to sweat a bit in his hand. "I assume that during the escape, Pickman somehow ended up on these grounds and made it to the place that you guys have marked as Pickman's Trail, right?" Cooper asked.

"That's right. But much of what happened during that little adventure was left off of our cute little historical plaque."

"Why's that?"

"Because sometimes history is ugly. Sometimes we'd rather forget about things the so-called innocent did and how it influenced history."

"What happened?"

Jack took another sip of soda and took a deep breath. Cooper picked up more of that talented storyteller vibe as he started up again.

"As Pickman and his crew were escaping, a gunfight broke out in the streets. Three of Pickman's crew were killed right there and then. The others, Pickman included, made it to the beach and headed for their ship. Pickman rounded up his daughter but, before they made it to the ship, she was shot in the back. From everything I've heard and read on the subject, this sent Pickman into a rage. He took his daughter up in one arm and started firing into the crowd. He went into a blind rampage. He was shot anywhere between three and five times and did not fall. He managed to get away from the crowd, escaping to this area and, as you guessed, into the caverns on these grounds."

Cooper took a moment to digest the violent story. "And this is all documented?"

"It is. In old newspaper clippings, a few random books, and good old word of mouth."

"Was he ever apprehended?"

"No one knows for sure," Jack answered. "But the thing that stands out about Pickman—the reason his legend didn't just quietly die away like so many other no-name pirates—was because of the threats he screamed at the locals as he was trying to escape."

"What kind of threats?"

"That even after he was dragged down to Hell, not even the Devil himself would stop him from killing every child in town if his daughter died."

THE COKES WERE DRAINED and the afternoon was cooling down. With the new information Jack Paulson had given him, Cooper could feel the night's task already pulling at him. He felt that old itch of being on the cusp of something monumental, of something that would give him yet another unfiltered glance into the unexplained. The old Cooper would have been positively wired.

But now, given the events of the past year of his life, it felt like a massive burden to carry.

He'd seen more than enough during his time in the field to solidify his belief in the supernatural, but he was always surprised and excited when he came across something new and unexpected. Surely the connections he had come across in the last thirty-six hours or so were leading him to just such an event. He could almost feel it pressing in around him, as if the air within a foot or so of his body was constantly being charged with a strange, electrical force.

Burden or not, he had no choice. He could only keep searching.

"You think you got enough for your book?" Jack asked him as they walked away from the picnic table and back towards Cooper's car.

"Oh yeah. More than enough. Thanks for your time."

"Of course."

Jack seemed to be thinking about something as they reached Cooper's car. He was looking to the right, toward the road that led to the campgrounds and trails. To Cooper, the old man looked deep in thought. Maybe he was imagining Douglass Pickman carrying his injured daughter into those woods.

"There's one other thing you might want to know," Jack said suddenly.

"What's that?"

"As you know, the caverns were closed several years back because the terrain further down was too treacherous. People were even slipping on the stairs with railings installed. We got two broken arms and a dislocated hip out of a few tourists. It got pretty nasty. The ceilings were starting to crumble in a few places, too. So it was an obvious decision to close the place down."

"I sense a *but* coming on," Cooper said.

Jack nodded and gave another grin. "*But*...among myself and a few of the other tour guides, we were almost glad to see the caverns close. I know it sounds stupid, but there was something about that place that never seemed right. I won't go so far as to say it was haunted or anything, but there was a feeling...I don't know how to describe it."

"Was it just the guides that felt it?"

"Oh not at all," Jack said. "We had at least thirty or so tourists over a five year period freak out when they were down there. And it wasn't just from pressure or claustrophobia. People were saying that they felt a tugging at their clothes and weird voices whispering in their ears. There was one lady that even said that she clearly heard a man say, '*I'll kill your children.*' Keep in mind that the guides never revealed the unsightly parts of Pickman's story to the groups we took down. No one really wants to hear that sort of stuff before you lead them down into a deep dark hole in the ground."

"Yeah, I guess not."

"You can decide whether or not to include that in your book on your own, I guess. Just don't use my name."

"Of course," Cooper said. "Now, as far as any other information, would you happen to have any maps of the caverns down there? Like any sort of actual schematics, layouts, anything like that?"

"You mean like a map of the actual cavern system?"

"Yes sir."

"Not that I know of. And even if there were, I'd highly suggest you not go down there even if you could. It's dangerous and, if I might be so honest, creepy as hell."

Cooper didn't bother hiding the disappointment from his face. "Well again, thanks for your help."

"No problem."

Cooper got into his car and pulled out of the visitor center parking lot. He looked back in his rearview and wasn't surprised to see Jack Paulson standing in the same place. He stood motionless, watching Cooper's car head back toward the beach as if he didn't quite trust the man that was driving it.

TWENTY

C ooper spent the rest of that afternoon in his motel room, browsing the internet for more information on Douglass Pickman while waiting for night to fall. He didn't find much, and what he *did* find was just different variations of what Jack Paulson had already told him. What Cooper found most interesting of all was that, after the events of Pickman's escape into the caverns, the locals were thought to have blocked the cave's entrance off. This was done even though none of those locals ever found Pickman or his daughter.

Cooper assumed this meant that Pickman had either found some other way out of the caverns and escaped the area, or he had died in there with his daughter.

When dusk fell, Cooper took a quick shower and drove to Mary Guthrie's house. He caught glimpses of the sun's last glimmering rays on the ocean between the beach houses and motels he passed on the way. Part of him wanted to slow down, maybe to park the car and sit on the beach to watch the day come to a close. Everything in the last two days had happened so fast, including his reunion and subsequent departure from Stephanie. Maybe it would do him some good to slow down.

Yet, of the many things that had changed about him since his disappearance a little less than a year ago, there were a few things that had remained very much the same. Chief among them was his aversion to sentiment. He'd never been a very emotional person, so things like beautiful sunsets and lost loves didn't usually stir much in him. That was one thing that his time away had apparently not changed about him.

The sunset and deep inner thoughts of all that he had been through would have to wait for some other time. If he planned to live life in constant motion, moving from place to place to help people like the Blackstocks, he was sure he'd find plenty of time for reflection.

He arrived at Mary Guthrie's house at 8:50, just as the last hues of sunlight were fading from the sky. The horizon was dark purple, tinged little spikes of almost poisonous-looking pink. It looked like a large bruise over the ocean.

When Mary answered the door, she looked both excited and fearful. It was a peculiar look to see on the face of a woman that was nearing sixty; it made her look younger in the eyes, but older everywhere else on her face. Cooper couldn't help but wonder if she was regretting her decision to let him come over.

"Come on in," she said, ushering him inside without much enthusiasm.

"Are you sure?" he asked, pausing at her doorway. "You're still up for this?"

"Of course, of course. Come on in."

He did as she asked, stepping through the doorway and into a small foyer. The colors in the foyer were bright and beachy, clearly having recently been cleaned and decorated for the vacationers that would be occupying the house in the coming months. There was even a decorative wooden sign along the foyer wall featuring flip flops and a beach umbrella that said *Welcome to the Beach!*

"Are you sure you still want to do this?" he asked before stepping through the door.

"You already asked me that."

"I know. I'm just making sure. Most people wouldn't be so willing to dive into it."

"I'm used to it. I'll be fine. What about you? Are you sure you're still up for it?"

He was...and maybe a little too much. Whether he wanted to admit it to himself or not, he'd missed the electric thrill of knowing he might be on the verge of interacting with something that existed beyond the rigid structures of the natural world.

"Absolutely," he finally said.

As she led him deeper into the house, Cooper noticed at once just how quiet the house was. There was no TV on in the background, no music. Even the crashing lull of the ocean through the walls seemed to be more muffled than usual.

He followed Mary straight through a hallway and into her kitchen. They sat down at her kitchen table where she already had the bag of Scrabble tiles out. They looked to have been randomly dumped from the bag, making a sloppy pile in the center of the table. It looked like children had been at play rather than the scene of a paranormal investigation in the making.

"How does this work?" Cooper asked. "Do you just ask them if they feel like talking?"

"No. Usually, they do as they please. Most of the time, they'll talk if they see the Scrabble tiles out. It's as if they know what I want ahead of time."

"And it doesn't scare you?"

"It did the first few times," she said with a smile. She considered her answer carefully and then continued. "I felt like I was maybe getting involved in something that I wasn't supposed to be messing with, you know? I'm not a religious or spiritual person by nature, but I do know that there is evil in the world and that things out of our sight and control probably shouldn't be tampered with."

"A good philosophy to live by," Cooper said.

He didn't bother adding in his own philosophy, one that he had not come to understand until about two years ago, after that haunting experience in a hospital room in Richmond, Virginia. That philosophy was that if there *was* evil and darkness in the world, there was also sufficient light to balance it out. At least that's where he was currently leaning.

"Given everything you and your lady friend told me about your history," Mary said, "I assume you've never really lived by those rules, though. Right?"

Cooper smiled, not quite sure how to respond. He had done a lot of self-reflection since reappearing eight months ago and had discovered some things about himself that had come as quite a surprise. He had yet to voice any of these things to anyone and found himself anxious to get them out.

Did it really matter if the first person he spoke some of these things to was a stranger?

He didn't think so.

Besides that, he and Stephanie had not told Mary very much at all. They'd only given her the bare bones. But he supposed that was more than enough information for Mary to make general assumptions.

"I was very cocky and sure of myself not too long ago," Cooper finally answered. "My book was being gobbled up by the paranormal community, but it was also getting respect from some mainstream outlets as well. And the thing that got me all of that attention was my fascination with those very things you feel we shouldn't mess with—trying to communicate with the other side and all of that."

"Do you think there *is* another side?" Mary asked.

"I do."

"So you believe in an afterlife?"

"Yes."

"How about Heaven and Hell?" She asked the question slowly, as if testing each word to make sure she wasn't crossing some sort of personal line with him.

"Yes, I do."

"And if you believe in Heaven, I assume you believe in God?"

"I do...and quite frankly, it's been a fairly recent development. With all due respect, though, I'm not here to discuss my personal theology."

"I apologize. But do you mind if I ask...do you personally believe that the afterlife and Heaven and Hell are all part of the same sort of system?"

"I don't know," he said. Admitting it hurt him a bit. After all he had been through, before, during, and after his disappearance, he still had no idea what all of his efforts had been for. He had always thought there was more to the world than what human senses could take in—some other realm or dimension just behind a veil thinner than paper. Over the years, he'd come to understand that certain humans could sometimes poke holes in that veil and peek to the other side. The questions that had plagued him and sent him down the very strange path his career had taken him on, though, was what could be seen on that other side.

And, beyond that, what sort of holes were beings on the other side poking in that very same veil?

And now he had his fairly new and very shaky faith to try to ground it all on, but even that didn't seem like enough at times. But that was certainly not something he wanted to get into with Mary Guthrie.

"Well how do you feel about what we're about to do?" she asked him. "This thing with my Scrabble tiles...is that dangerous in any way?"

"There's no way to be certain. But based on past experiences, I don't think so."

"I use what I have," she said, with a smile. "I thought about going out to get a Ouija board and try that out...but the idea of it scared me."

"It's a good thing you didn't," Cooper said. He was glad that the topic of conversation had shifted and he wanted to make sure it kept going in the desired direction. So he did his best to play his part.

"Why is that?" Mary asked.

"I don't know how it happened, but Ouija boards got this innocent sort of board game reputation somewhere in the last fifty years or so. The truth of the matter is that if you use them in a place where there is a real, legitimate dark presence, they can be dangerous. They can serve as literal doorways."

Mary's face grew very serious and alarmed. Cooper had never been good at filtering himself. He had to constantly keep reminding himself that not everyone was as accustomed to the supernatural as he was. He could be off-putting to say the least. Stephanie's absence was proof of that.

"You've seen this?" Mary asked. "This...*evil?*"

"I have," he said coldly. The memory of it still chilled him years later. He saw the eighteen-year-old in the hospital bed, screeching in a voice that was clearly not his own. He saw the terrified doctors, the weeping nurses, and then the preacher with the Bible in his hands.

Yes, he had seen evil. And he had also seen what kept it at bay.

Still, even after witnessing evil flee at the simple reading of scripture and the name of Christ, Cooper knew that the darkness had its hooks, its claws, its sharp edges. Faith came in all shapes and sizes, all kinds of religions and superstitions. But the same was true of evil and darkness.

What made no sense to Cooper in that moment, sitting with Mary in her kitchen, was that he had gone back looking for similar things time after time.

"I'm sorry," Mary said. "I didn't mean to pry."

"It's okay. It does me some good to talk about all of this. Especially now."

He could sense her wanting to ask more questions about his past. Part of him wished that she would so he could verbalize some of it, hoping to uncover some hidden truth he had yet to realize. But another part of him wasn't quite ready to look into the darker shadows of his past—especially not with an older woman he didn't know.

Instead, they shared a string of polite conversation about the upcoming tourist season. As they spoke, Mary put on a pot of coffee. The conversation eventually led Cooper to sharing details about his day and what he had discovered about Douglass Pickman. Mary knew very little about the more intimate history, having only heard the whitewashed version of it. The tale seemed to make her uneasy. She started to look at the Scrabble tiles as if they were poisonous insects rather than a prop from a board game.

Yet as ten o'clock approached, Mary sat down at the table with a cup of coffee. Slowly, she reached out for the tiles and sifted through a few of them playfully. The noise of their clattering on the table filled the house and was eerie beyond explanation. Cooper watched as she started to flip them all over, letters-up. He joined in and they sat there with the tiles between them, pushed to the edge of the table as if awaiting a third person to start a game.

"Does this help?" he asked.

"What's that?"

"Us...playing with the tiles."

"I don't know. I was hoping the sound of someone playing with them would maybe bring them out. It seems to always work with Amy."

Working together, they flipped the rest of the tiles over. When that was done, the house was silent again. The hushed whisper of the ocean outside was like a ragged breathing through the walls, as if the world was gasping for air.

"That's it?" Cooper asked, his eyes still on the tiles.

"Yes. Of course, now we just have to wait for them to come."

Cooper nodded, but even as she spoke, he started to get a very familiar feeling. It was one that he had felt so often in his past that it had become almost common to him. It was the feeling of a slight chill in the air, accompanied with the feeling of being watched. He felt something very close to a mild pins-and-needles sensation in his fingers, groin, and neck. He'd always supposed there was an unknown form of electricity to it all as the human body and its natural state prepared for something very unnatural.

He looked to Mary and saw that she was beginning to glance anxiously around the kitchen. She looked uncomfortable, but not exactly scared. Cooper looked at her arms and saw the smallest signs of goosebumps. She was feeling it, too, whether she knew it or not.

Cooper was pretty sure that Amy and her friends were here.

With a shaky sigh, Mary turned towards the open kitchen and adjoining living room.

"You feel it?" Mary asked him.

Cooper only nodded, wanting to keep as quiet as possible while the strange new energy within the room manifested itself.

"Amy?" Mary asked, her voice light and wavering. She managed to keep her voice friendly and pleasant despite the obvious edge of fear that supported it all. "Are you and your little friends here for a visit? I have a friend of my own here that would very much like to speak with you."

A minute passed. The room was silent and still, yet Cooper continued to feel that familiar sensation. He was certain that there was *something* here with them. The room was growing slightly colder and he started to feel something like cobwebs on his arm—more signs of a supernatural presence or event on the horizon.

Based on past experiences, the slightness of the sensation indicated that whatever force was here with them was a harmless one. In cases where the unseen force or entity was malevolent, there was usually a weird and unsettling feeling in the stomach of anyone within the room. Some people also reported a scent similar to charred bread or thick dust.

But Cooper was not picking up any of that.

What I wouldn't give for some of my old equipment, he thought to himself. *An EMF detector, a voice recorder, or even just a thermal imager would be incredible right now.*

He took a sip of his coffee to calm himself, knowing that something important and probably supernatural was about to happen.

Cooper almost opened his mouth to call for Amy as well.

But before he got the chance, the Scrabble tiles started to move.

TWENTY-ONE

There was nothing dramatic about it and nothing at all frightening. The tiles just moved, sorted by invisible hands, and were scattered softly across the table. Most of them were turned over while others were brushed aside.

Cooper watched, fascinated. He was very aware of the smile on his face and saw no good reason to force it away. These were the types of moments he lived for. These moments were what had shaped his life not too long ago, and the thrill had apparently not faded. It was so familiar that he drew comfort from it.

As he watched, two tiles were pushed out across the table. They were then scooted side by side, forming a simple word.

HI.

"Hello," Cooper said, trying to sound serious and friendly rather than excited and awed. Oddly enough, he did not feel foolish as he spoke to the invisible presence. "Are you Amy?"

The **HI** was pulled down to the rest of the pile of tiles and the rest of them were sorted through. Again, two more tiles were pushed away from the others and placed side by side to spell a word near the edge of the table.

This one was **NO.**

"What's your name?" Cooper asked.

He watched the tiles move as if by magic again. He resisted the urge to reach out and feel the cold spot that he was certain would be at the end of the table. He looked across to Mary and saw that she was smiling, but nervously.

After a few seconds, Cooper got his answer.

KEVIN ELEVEN YRS OLD

Kevin Owens, Cooper thought.

Cooper's body went cold all over. His thoughts turned to Kevin's parents, having just lost their son. He thought of how they'd left their home by the beach and headed somewhere else to escape the recent death of their son.

If they only knew, he thought.

"Nice to meet you Kevin."

He almost added *Sorry about what happened to you,* but he wasn't sure how the ghost of a recently deceased child might handle a reminder of their death. When dealing with the supernatural, this was the sort of conversational etiquette one needed to be aware of at all times. The thought nearly made Cooper chuckle.

Mary then spoke up, speaking softly. "Is Amy here, Kevin?"

They watched the tiles move for another thirty seconds or so until they received an answer.

NOT RIGHT NOW.

"Kevin," Cooper said, "I'm trying to find out why a little boy died a few years ago. His parents are very sad and miss him. And right now, there are very strange things happening in their home. Their son's name is Henry. Henry Blackstock. Do you know him?"

The letters moved again, a bit quicker now as the ghost of Kevin Owens got more familiar with the tiles. There was a confidence in the way the tiles moved now, clicking and clacking against the table musically.

NOW BUT NOT BEFORE

The answer was loaded with mystery and begged more questions. But Cooper was pretty sure he knew what it meant: Kevin had recently become acquainted with Henry Blackstock, probably after his death.

And while he certainly appreciated Mary's approach at handling what seemed to be the ghosts of children with kid's gloves, Cooper had never quite operated that way. Ghosts were fickle. You could ask them their favorite colors and songs all day long but in Cooper's experience, they usually wanted to talk about more serious matters.

"Do you know what happened to you?" Cooper asked.

After a few more seconds of clattering tiles, the answer appeared.

DROWNED

"When you drowned, were you close to this house?" Cooper asked. "Were there tall black rocks sticking out of the water nearby?"

The tiles moved once again, with their same clacking music. This time, they formed the word **YES**

"And did someone pull you into the water?"

NO BUT I SAW A MAN

The tiles were moving faster now. Cooper was pretty sure that they were moving *too* fast. He didn't think they were being moved by ghostly fingers anymore. He'd always wondered if ghosts—poltergeists in particular—were able to move objects not with the physical movements of their phantom bodies but with some form of emotional thought. If so, he felt certain he was witnessing exactly that with Mary's Scrabble tiles.

"Kevin?" Mary asked. "Have you been here in my house before?"

YES

Mary's smile faltered a bit and Cooper didn't blame her. He tried to think of what questions he should ask in order to get the information he needed. But his thoughts were interrupted by the scattering of tiles again.

He watched them dance and slide. This time, Kevin formed

one word first and then two others underneath it. When he was done, the letters created a very brief message.

BYE

NOW AMY

The tiles sat still and motionless as Cooper and Mary stared at the message. Cooper was afraid it meant that the weird little session was over, but Mary was looking skeptically around the room as if she knew better.

"He's gone," Cooper said, no longer feeling the coolness in the air. It was a hard sensation to describe. To Cooper, it felt as if someone had placed a thin layer of wet paper towels on the back of his neck for several minutes and then removed them.

But as soon as he was certain Kevin had gone, he felt it again. This time, the sensation was a bit more present—a bit more *there.* If he'd had his thermal imager, he was pretty sure he would have been able to pick up the figure of a small person standing a few feet away from them.

Cooper gave Mary a quick wave to get her attention and then nodded to the tiles. She looked down just as they started to move again.

HI MARY

"Amy?" Mary asked.

The tiles were moving slower now, back to a normal speed. They were moved with a child's care as they were sorted out, three tiles pushed to the side to spell out **YES.**

"I have a friend here to visit you," Mary said. "Is that okay?"

Amy quickly spelled out **GOOD.**

When Cooper spoke again, he understood how surreal this truly was. He was essentially speaking to a stack of Scrabble tiles. But he had seen and felt more than enough in the last ten years or so to know that there *was* some supernatural force standing by the end of the table and manipulating the tiles. Again, he found himself badly wanting a camera...anything to document this amazing experience. He had his phone but he feared the movement and overall process of filming the event would somehow cheapen it. It also might drive Amy away.

"Amy," Cooper said. "I asked your friend Kevin about a boy named Henry Blackstock. Do you know him?"

The tiles moved slowly at first, but then began to pick up speed. By the time Amy was done with what was the longest message they had seen during their session, there was an obvious urgency to the message.

YES HE DROWNED was spelled out and then pushed to one side of the table. Then, on the other side, the one closest to Mary, the tiles moved around and spelled out another message—one that made Cooper freeze for a moment.

HE SAW DARK WATER.

"What do you mean by dark water?"

HIS WATER

"Henry's water?" Cooper asked, confused.

The tiles were flipped through and scattered again. It was now very apparent that they were being moved by much more than just phantom fingers. As they were sorted through, some of them moved with such speed that they seemed to be a blur as they were moved. A few were bounced from the table and into the floor.

NO THE BAD MANS WATER

The tiles were scattered, rearranged, and then once more spelled out DARK WATER.

"Amy, I don't know what that—"

He didn't get a chance to finish before the tiles started moving again. They moved with such speed and prominent clicks against the table that it was obvious that Amy was trying to interrupt him. Maybe it was her way of telling him to shut up already.

Cooper snapped his mouth shut and watched the tiles move as they spelled out a series of messages that made his heart grow cold.

HE KNOWS U R HERE

This message was swiped back into the pile, leaving a blank table for only a few seconds before Amy started spelling out another one. This one read: **HES ANGRY WANTS TO HURT**

"Who?" Cooper asked. "Who does he want to hurt?"

DROWNS KIDS IN DARK WATER

"How can I stop him?"

DONT KNOW

"Amy, was the dark water the last thing you saw?"

Here, the movement in the tile stopped for a moment, as if Amy was taking the moment to think. It felt like the very room itself was pausing to take a breath. After a handful of seconds, the tiles started moving again as Amy gave her answer.

YES

Cooper wondered if, like Henry Blackstock, her body had remained undiscovered.

"Is Henry with you?" Cooper asked. "Not here tonight, but wherever it is that you are the rest of the time."

Her answer came quickly as the tiles began to move with that eerie speed again.

YES BUT NOT NOW

Mary spoke up next. Cooper was surprised to find that she was close to tears. Her bottom lip trembled slightly as she spoke. "Amy...where are you? Where do you and your friends stay?"

DARK PLACE WITH BAD MAN

This message was swiped aside and then the entire pile of tiles seemed to separate slightly. Cooper watched as one of the blank tiles was selected and then slid all the way over to him, directly beside his coffee cup. This was followed by the spelling out of a repeated message, placed in front of him so he'd know the message was meant specifically for him.

HE KNOWS U R HERE

That was swiped away and quickly replaced with **HE HATES U**

"He knows I'm trying to stop him," Cooper said.

YES

"Do you know his name?" he asked, certain that the bad man the little girl was referring to was Douglass Pickman.

NO

"Where is he? Where can I find him? Is it in a cave?"

The tiles moved with blinding speed. It made sense, he supposed, as he'd just asked three rapid-fire questions. As he watched the tiles move around, Cooper became aware of the air growing even colder. The room started to feel thick, as if the oxygen was slowly being sucked out of it.

From across the table, Mary whispered to him. "Do you feel that?"

He nodded, still watching as new words were spelled out one right after another.

DONT KNOW

COLD

NO LIGHT

DARK WATER

"What else can you tell me?" Cooper asked.

NO TIME HAVE TO GO

HES MAD

"Amy, please…"

The letters were being moved frantically now, the clicking of tiles against the table like the sound of someone typing frantically.

HELP HE HATES PLEASE DARK WA

But Amy was not able to finish her last message. The tiles exploded all across the table, some being flung across the room where they clattered against the wall and fell to the floor. One hit Cooper squarely in the face, bouncing into his lap to reveal an **O**.

Mary cried out and jumped back in her chair. She looked around the room frantically, as if she was looking for someone. There was a profound look of sadness on her face. When she looked to Cooper, he saw that she was terrified.

"That's never happened before," she said.

Cooper nodded slowly, looking around at the scattered

Scrabble tiles. He looked for hidden messages in them but could find none. He stood up, staring at the table where he had witnessed one of the oddest things he had ever seen.

"Are you okay?" he asked Mary.

"I think so." She thought about something for a while, looking through her sliding glass door and to the night-shrouded beach beyond. "Do you think the *he* Amy mentioned is this Pickman character you learned about?"

"I do."

"She made it sound like he pulled them under water somehow," Mary said, wiping a tear away from her cheek. "And now he's keeping them trapped in the dark with him."

She stifled back a weak sob that made Cooper think that, oddly enough, Mary had grown quite attached to Amy.

"It seems that way," Cooper agreed without much emotion.

Still looking out of the door and toward the ocean, Mary asked, "Do you think you can stop him?"

Cooper faced the sliding glass door and looked out to the beach as well. He stared towards the dark ocean, in the direction of where the black rocks broke through the water. He could not see them from where he stood. All he could see out there were the occasional white crests of waves, like fissures in the surface of the world.

Looking out into the darkness, he said: "I'm sure as hell going to try."

TWENTY-TWO

When Cooper returned to his hotel room, it was just after eleven o' clock. He looked at the bed skeptically, well aware that he was too wired to sleep. He had a plan in mind—an idea to potentially stop whatever it was that Douglass Pickman was up to—but it would be useless to start before morning. He sat on the edge of his bed and pulled out his phone.

He scrolled to Stephanie's number, his thumb hovering over her name. He was nearly certain that she wouldn't answer his call, but he didn't see the harm in trying. He was sure she was expecting him to at least *try* a few times.

He sent the call and listened as the phone rang twice before being picked up by her voice mail. He listened to the recorded message and almost stayed on the line to wait for the beep. But he killed the call, not even sure what sort of message he would leave.

As he sat in the quiet of the hotel room with its bland and perfectly square shapes to everything, Cooper came to a realization that he did not like at all.

For the first time in more than five or six years, he was legitimately frightened.

He had no expensive government-purchased equipment to help him.

He had no book or hidden agenda at the forefront of his mind to use as motivation.

All he had now was a set of frightened parents that had never truly stopped grieving for their dead child, unable to do so because of the ghosts that occasionally visited their house. Cooper understood that the desire to help someone other than himself was his only true driving motivation...and that scared him.

What if he failed? What if he found that after his disappearance, and without the aid of his old ego and drive, he could not face the unknown as he once had? He felt especially naked and useless without his government-funded equipment. What good could he do without his old technological fallbacks?

These were all heavy thoughts that seemed to make the motel room feel like a coffin. He stepped out of the room into the humid night. He breathed in the salt air and lingered outside of his door for a while before walking down to the parking lot. To the right of the lot, the motel was separated from the neighboring motel by a strip of sand-blasted asphalt. A fence ran along the length of this divide, meandering to the back of both buildings where it stopped at a wooden walkway that led out onto the beach.

Cooper followed this path and found the beach empty. In the pale moonlight, the sand almost seemed to glow for a moment. He walked out in his bare feet, reminded of how he had felt yesterday morning when he'd first stepped out onto this sand. It felt like two *weeks* ago rather than two days.

He looked out to the sea, trying to rationalize his fears. He had never fully understood the hold the ocean had on some people but as he watched it under the moonlight, he thought he understood it. From where he stood, the ocean seemed to go on forever. It appeared that way during daylight hours but at night, there was something different about it. At night, the ocean was a vast canopy of darkness that seemed to have swallowed up the rest of the world. Out near the horizon, that endless sheet of darkness seemed to promise limitless depth and things without end. In comparison, his fears about what he was planning to do seemed insignificant.

He knew how clichéd he looked—the lonely, troubled man staring blankly out to sea at night. But he was surprised to find that it helped. He thought of Pickman and of Mary Guthrie's Scrabble tiles as he stared into the shimmering darkness. Just another lost and wandering human staring out to the sea for answers and direction.

Dark water, he thought.

For a moment, it sounded like the crashing waves were speaking those words to him.

A chilled breeze swept through. The ocean droned on, offering its tired but enchanting lullaby. The water remained moving yet unmoving all at once. It was peaceful, it was—

Without warning, Cooper saw a perfect picture in his mind that took his breath away.

It came to the surface of his mind like a whale out there in the infinite darkness of the ocean, only to surface for a moment before plunging back into the deep.

Cooper caught the briefest glimpse of *something* in his mind but he wasn't sure what it was. This was not a vision, but the edge of some buried memory poking up through the shifting sand of his thoughts.

He saw flat terrain the color of rust and the shapes of boulders in the distance. He saw an endless vista of sky that was a faded shade of blue so light it was almost white. At the horizon, there was a delicate streak of purple that looked like it was dancing. It wavered in such a way that it appeared to be beckoning, telling him to come forward. Behind that there were faint ghost-like shapes, the peaks of what he thought to be enormous mountains.

There was uncertainty in that place, in the muted colors and the horizon that seemed to be pulling him forward. But there was also a sense of tremendous peace that he felt in every muscle of his body, every—

And then it was gone.

Cooper stood on the beach, eyes wide. He was holding his breath, concentrating with everything he had to get the image to come back.

No, not a vision, he thought, correcting himself again. *A memory.*

Then, with a certainty as large as the sea before him, another thought came.

That's where I was. That's where I went when I disappeared.

Cooper continued to stare out at the dark sea, hoping that it might trigger whatever had pushed that momentary memory to the surface. He tried dredging it back up but it was like trying to think of a word that was on the tip of his tongue but getting little assistance from the brain to be spoken.

Over the last several months, whenever he tried to find those memories, all he could come up with were images of the small town of Tilton, Kansas. Tilton was the last city he had visited before disappearing. Beyond that, he knew very little.

He remembered a teenage boy, but not his name. He remembered a junk yard and some weird fear that was linked to it. And lights...hadn't there been some sort of lights?

But that's where the memories ended.

After five minutes of this, Cooper grew frustrated. He was also suddenly very tired. He didn't know if it was the mental strain or the effect of the memory itself, but he was suddenly exhausted. With a final look to the sea and the white caps of the countless waves, Cooper turned around and walked back to his motel.

When he reached his room, he shook the sand from his feet and crawled into bed. He set the alarm clock for 5:30, knowing that tomorrow's events would be grueling and might take all day. He lay down in bed with the picture of that remembered place in his head, ebbing and flowing out of reach like the waves that crashed behind the motel.

Already, his memory of the place was starting to fade.

He looked to the red digital numbers of the clock, his eyes growing heavy. He faintly read the time, 11:51, and then let sleep claim him.

TWENTY-THREE

When the phone rang, Cooper snapped awake with a jerk. It was not the gentle purring of his cellphone, but the annoying blast of the motel phone on the bedside table. It was abrasive and almost comically loud, clanging like some prehistoric machine.

He sat up quickly, his thoughts in a jumbled mess. Had he called down to the desk for a wake-up call? He didn't think so. He was pretty sure he'd set the alarm clock.

The phone rang again. With blurry eyes, Cooper looked at the alarm clock and saw that it was 3:22.

Steph, he thought.

He *hoped.*

He answered the phone in the middle of its far-too-loud third ring. He was still so jostled and sluggish from sleep that he nearly dropped the receiver as he brought it to his ear. His heart thrummed in his chest like a wild animal, still spooked from being jarred so rudely awake.

"Hello?"

The voice on the other end was female, but it wasn't Stephanie.

"I'm sorry to call so late," the woman said. Her voice was

thick and wavering with fright and panic. "It's Jenny Blackstock. We...I...I think we might need your help."

The sleep that had been clinging to him slid off instantly, as if it had been nothing more than a cheap sheet.

"What is it? Are you okay?"

"Yeah, we're fine. It's just...I don't know...something happened. It's worse than it's ever been. We don't know what to do and—"

In the background, Cooper heard something clatter to the floor. Immediately after this, he heard Sam Blackstock's voice yelling *"Get out!"*

Cooper was now very much awake. More than that, he felt a surge of adrenaline spiking through him. And somewhere further back, he felt something akin to anger—anger directed toward an entity he was now almost certain was Douglass Pickman.

"I can be there in ten minutes," Cooper said.

He hung up the phone so fast that he cut off Jenny Blackstock as she gave him a shaky "Thank you."

———————————

THE FIRST THING Cooper noticed when he pulled up to the Blackstocks's house was that every light inside had been turned on. It looked like a weird, misplaced lighthouse in comparison to the darkened houses surrounding it. As he walked to the front door, Cooper looked to the left and could just barely make out the murky shape of Mary Guthrie's house six houses down.

He wondered if Amy and Kevin had ever gone back to visit her after their little Scrabble encounter.

The front door to the Blackstocks's house opened up as Cooper was walking up the porch stairs. Jenny stood aside, letting him come in. Her eyes were red and puffy from crying and she looked exhausted. Her hair was in sleep-stressed shambles. She tucked a loose strand of it behind her ear as she greeted him.

"Is everything okay?" Cooper asked.

"We're fine, I guess. I don't think they can hurt us. Can they?"

"Who?"

She shrugged and said just two words. When she said it, she did so with a broken nervous laugh. It chilled Cooper. He thought it was the sound of someone that was losing their grip on sanity.

"The ghosts."

"Are they still here?" Cooper asked.

Jenny looked surprised for a moment. Cooper assumed that she had been expecting a bit of disbelief or hesitancy on his part. His eagerness to accept her word on such a wild claim had taken her by surprise.

"Yes," she said. "Upstairs. Come on."

He followed her up the stairs and could sense the changes in the house right away. The atmosphere was drastically different from when he had last been in their house. The air was thicker and chilled. While the cold air in Mary Guthrie's house had made the hairs on his neck stand on end, the one in the Blackstock's house made him shiver. He'd experienced this sort of coldness a few times in the past. On each of those occasions, things of monumental importance had occurred.

He felt a tightness in his chest as they neared the top of the stairs, and the world seemed to sway a bit.

Cooper found himself mentally filing through each case where he had experienced such a dramatic shift in the atmosphere of a house but wouldn't allow himself to get distracted. He sensed that things were happening far too fast in the Blackstock home, and he had very little time.

"Where's Sam?" he asked as they neared the stairs.

"He's on the back porch, watching the beach. He swears he

saw someone standing down there after all of this started happening."

They finally came to the top of the stairs. Cooper paused before walking into the living room. He took in the scene as best as he could, trying to make sense of what was happening before he focused solely on the fact that there was *definitely* another presence in the room with them.

The living room and the adjoining kitchen were littered with fragments of broken plates and glasses. The handle to a coffee mug was on the living room carpet two feet in front of Cooper. Two pictures had been thrown from the walls and a few refrigerator magnets were scattered across the floor. The kitchen cupboards were open and the silverware drawer was in shambles. A few forks lay on the floor, and a single spoon rested on the other side of the kitchen.

Jenny pointed to a small glass that was lying by the foot of the couch, partially shattered. "That hit Sam in the side of the head. It didn't hurt him—not really—but it scared us."

Cooper slowly walked across the room, towards the small dining area. He looked through the sliding glass door and saw Sam standing on the porch. He was positioned at the top of the stairs, looking out to the sea. Cooper looked in that direction as well but saw nothing beyond the back yard, despite the patio lights.

Cooper turned away from the window and walked back into the living room, trying to get a feel for the other presence. He didn't feel anything immediately threatening, but there was certainly something in the house that was darker than what he had experienced in Mary's home.

"What happened?" he asked Jenny. "Tell me as much as you can."

Before she spoke, she glanced cautiously around the living room, as if she were waiting for some unseen assailant to come out of hiding. "At first, it was just like all of the other times. We heard the laughing kids and Sam got out of bed right away.

Within a few seconds, the laughter sounded more like crying. This one...well, it was a boy this time and we...we..."

Jenny stopped there, looking to the shattered plates, glass, magnets and other debris on the floor.

"You thought it might be Henry," Cooper said.

"Yeah. Isn't that stupid?"

"No, it isn't. Not at all."

Jenny shook the thought away and did her best to go on. "We came out here and the laughter or crying or whatever it was...well, it was right here in the room with us. Usually, it sort of fades out, but it stayed this time. We asked if the laughing boy was Henry. We didn't get an answer. But the noise tapered off and the room got really cold." She trembled a bit and shook her head. "Like really cold. I can't even explain it."

"Did you hear anything other than laughter and crying?"

"Yeah. It was like a bad radio reception, only without the static. That's the only way I know how to describe it. We heard a few kids and it sounded like their noises were coming in through a sort of filter. That was before all of the plates and glasses started coming out of the cupboards."

"You didn't *see* anything while it was happening?"

"Just the stuff flying out of the cupboards and off the kitchen counter."

"But no kids?"

"No, I didn't see anything like that. But Sam started yelling at something. He said he saw a man leaving the house, leaving off the back porch and heading for the beach."

"Was he able to describe him?"

Jenny shook her head. "He said all he saw was black. Just the black shadowy shape of a man."

"Did he—" Cooper started, but he stopped before he could fully form the question.

The room went frigid in the space of a second. For a moment, Cooper felt like someone had taken the air right out of his lungs.

It was like being punched in the stomach, only without the punch.

With it, there came the smell of pungent salt water.

"What is that?" Jenny asked. "Do you feel it?"

Cooper nodded and started looking around the house. Somewhere off in the distance, he thought he heard a child screaming.

"Did you hear that?" he asked in a whisper so low that he barely made a sound at all.

Jenny nodded, her eyes wide. She was crying, a single tear rolling down her cheek. She looked absolutely terrified as she brought her hand to her mouth. Her body was shaking. Cooper knew the feeling well. Before he had grown accustomed to these sorts of things, he'd experienced it several times. He was very familiar with the feeling of his body wanting to retreat in one hundred different directions at once.

"I hate to ask you this," Cooper said, "but does it sound like Henry?"

Jenny seemed to think about it for a moment and then shook her head. "No. But my God, what is that *cold*? And the smell. Do you smell it?"

As if in response to her question, the dining room table vibrated next to them. They both turned that way and when they did, the chair closest to Cooper begin to rise into the air.

Again, Cooper heard a child's scream. It was just like Jenny had described—like hearing a crackled voice through a bad radio reception.

Cooper tried to understand it, sure that it was saying something. But as he concentrated, the chair was suddenly thrown towards him. It came with very little force, but it struck him on the waist hard enough to make him stumble.

Jenny cried out as Cooper went to his left knee. He stood up right away, fully expecting another chair to come sailing at him.

Instead, he received something that he was fully unprepared for. It was something he had experienced only once before in his decade or so in the field, and he had hoped to never experience it again.

There was a split second where he saw a figure standing directly in front of him. It came out of nowhere, like appearing from behind a dropped sheet. And as soon as Cooper saw it, the figure was rushing at him, its edges nothing more than blurs of motion that trailed out in transparent waves behind it.

Just before the figure struck him, he saw its face.

It was the same face that he had seen on the black rocks the night before, right down to the rotted teeth.

The apparition passed through Cooper, sending a spike of frigid energy through him. Every nerve in his body responded, trying to keep him warm, only to find that the frigid feeling was not anything natural to defend against. For the second time that night, Cooper felt the sensation of pins and needles, only this time it was through his entire body.

It brought with it a simple message, echoed with voiceless words that sounded like low rumbling thunder creeping across a deserted field on a summer evening.

GO AWAY!

Cooper went to the floor, his stomach clenching and his heart feeling as if it had been pierced with an icicle. He clenched his teeth and let out a moan, trying to keep some aspect of the apparition inside of him. He needed to feel it, to understand it… it was something he had not known to do when it had happened to him years ago.

But now with the fear pushed to the very fringes of his mind and a chilly determination gripping him, Cooper felt the presence inside of him as something other than the simple coldness of its being.

He saw flashes of what the figure was. And for the briefest of moments, he could actually sense what it felt.

The entity was full of hate…a blinding rage that made Cooper cringe. He saw a large ship right out of the history books, complete with ragged sails and groaning wooden curves.

He then saw a little girl and a crowd of people on a dusty street. Many of the people were shouting. Some had guns.

He then saw blood, the darkness of a tunnel, and water so black it looked like oil.

Dark water.

And around it all, there were the children. The screaming children that reached out for something to grab onto as ocean water poured into their mouths, into their lungs—

That was enough.

Cooper let out a brief scream and allowed the last remnants of the apparition to exit his body. He felt it go like some large insect that had landed on his chest and crawled around for a while, suddenly taking off on misshapen wings.

He coughed twice, feeling like there was something that needed to come up. But once he caught his breath again, he was fine. There was a bit of pressure in his chest but after a few moments, that dissipated, too.

There was a hand on his shoulder that he realized belonged to Jenny Blackstock.

"My God, what happened?" she asked.

Cooper made it to his knees and then, using the side of the dining table, managed to make it to his feet. The chill inside of him had already started to thaw and he could sense an immediate change in the room.

"I was attacked."

"By what?"

Cooper caught his breath and then took a seat at the table. He rubbed at his temples, feeling a headache starting to bloom. There was too much going on in there right now. He heard Pickman's demand (*GO AWAY*) and the screaming of those children, all layered together.

"Go get Sam," Cooper said. "He'll want to hear this, too."

He had made up his mind that the Blackstocks should know the basics of what he thought was happening.

"Is everything okay?" Jenny asked.

"I don't know. But the man Sam is watching for on the beach just left. His name is Douglass Pickman and he just passed right through me."

"Did he hurt you?"

"It wasn't pleasant, but I'm okay. He just wanted to scare me, and he did a very good job. But I'm not going anywhere just yet."

"One second," Jenny said. Her face was pale as she hurried for the sliding glass door.

Cooper watched her open it, leaving it cracked as she went out to her husband. The soft sounds of the night surf crashing on the shore crept in and, until Jenny and Sam came back in, Cooper could have sworn he heard Pickman speaking through it, repeating that same message.

GO AWAY!

"Not just yet," Cooper whispered to the room.

But God help him, he couldn't remember the last time he'd been so scared.

TWENTY-FOUR

After leaving the Blackstocks's house at 4:25, Cooper headed to the far end of Kill Devil Hills, beyond the area known as Jockey's Ridge, to where the only thing that seemed beach-like were the billboards. The beach houses and unique businesses and establishments became less frequent, allowing room for more depressingly familiar names: Starbucks, Texaco, Walmart, and McDonald's.

Cooper drove through a McDonald's drive thru, pitying the poor girl behind the window that had to work the early morning shift. He ordered two sausage biscuits and a large coffee. Within a few bites of the first biscuit, he realized that he wasn't going to be able to eat; he was too nervous, too frightened. The coffee, however, went down just fine. He drank it black and it calmed him a bit. He knew he should be tired, but his body was filled with frantic energy as dawn crept its way toward the beach.

He sipped on his coffee as he drove half a mile down the road to a twenty-four hour Walmart. Walking toward the entrance under the glow of the big, white letters along the front of the building, he felt like he was walking in a dream. Was this really happening? Was he seriously about to do this? The electric lights of retail seemed to suggest that it was very real and yes, he was indeed about to do this.

Cooper went inside quickly, afraid that if he gave himself enough time, he might very well talk himself out of what he had planned. Coffee in hand, he went about his shopping and hoped he looked somewhat normal. He passed only a few other shoppers as he made his way through the aisles. While the items in his basket probably seemed suspicious, he thought they would likely go unnoticed by anyone that happened to be in a Walmart at such an ungodly hour.

Even the cashier seemed not to care; she was a twenty-something blonde with a dark tan, bored out of her mind, and likely only motivated by visions of going to the beach in about six hours. She rang up his purchases with as little conversation as possible. She looked at Cooper only briefly, with the dead glance of people that worked the early morning hours.

Cooper wheeled his purchases out to his car in a shopping cart and threw them in the back seat. There was a loud clatter as everything jostled together—the flashlight, the axe, the crowbar, the shovel, the box of garbage bags, the bottles of water, the box of salt, and the sledgehammer.

He took one of the plastic bags from his shopping excursion to the front of the car and sat it in the passenger seat. He removed one of the bottles of water and the flashlight batteries. As he held the batteries in one hand, he also removed the salt from the bag and looked at it with a slight sense of distrust. It was the closest thing to his old equipment he had allowed himself to consider and he *truly* hoped it would work.

If it didn't, he thought he might be in for some very big trouble.

It made him think about what might happen if he died in the next few hours—which, he guessed, was a possibility. At some point, he supposed Stephanie would try to reach out to him, if for no other reason than just to check on him. And even if

Stephanie remained in the shadows, Jenny and Sam Blackstock might wonder what happened to him after he'd told them everything he knew about Douglass Pickman.

There were connections everywhere…from the Blackstocks to Mary Guthrie, and even to Jack Paulson, the lore-wielding ex-tour guide at the visitor's center. If he died, Cooper thought *someone* might eventually put things together.

He tried to imagine what the people he had once worked for might think if they discovered that, not only had he resurfaced after disappearing for nine months, but that he had *really* died while doing an investigation upon his return. The very idea and irony of it made him smile. Cooper knew they'd be more interested to know that the investigation had not been for personal gain. It wasn't for a book, an interview, or publicity. It had been to try to help grieving parents move on and, in the process, to potentially prevent the deaths of other kids in the future.

It was the first time he had given any real thought to the idea that, by using his real name in these investigations (if there was another to follow this one), the people he had once worked for would probably find him before too long. What they might do to him once he was discovered was a toss-up. They'd either welcome him with open arms despite his having nearly blown their cover publicly on multiple occasions, or take him in a darkened alley and put a bullet in his head.

Cooper wasn't particularly interested in either scenario.

With a sigh, he cranked the car and pulled out of his parking spot.

In doing so, he nearly ran over the man standing in front of his car.

Cooper let out a shout of surprise and slammed on the brakes. All of the equipment in the back seat clattered to the floorboard in jangled commotion. Cooper looked at the man, wondering where he had come from. He had not been there thirty seconds ago. Looking at him, Cooper wondered if the man was drunk. He was standing perfectly still, seemingly unfazed by the fact that he had almost been run down by a car.

The man was dressed in a button-down shirt with a tacky Hawaiian print and khaki shorts. He was slightly overweight and his thick legs looked ghastly white in the car's headlights. He was partially bald and the hair he *did* have looked as if it had not been washed in quite some time.

Cooper looked out to the man furiously and made a sideways waving gesture. *Get out of the way!*

The man shrugged and actually stepped closer to the car. He reached out a hand and touched the hood. Furious now, Cooper rolled down his window and poked his head out.

"Get out of the way, man. What are you doing?"

The man frowned but did not move. "I was hoping you'd recognize me," he said.

"I have no idea who you are," Cooper said, doing his best to keep his anger in check. "Now get out of my way, please."

The man stood his ground and Cooper decided that he had no time for this sort of craziness. Ignoring the man completely, Cooper shifted the car into reverse. When his foot touched the pedal, he felt the man's hand on his shoulder.

Cooper not only hit the brake, but he had to bite back a scream of surprise.

How'd he move that fast? How'd he move from the front of the car to the door that fast?

The question went through Cooper's mind like a bullet. Behind that question was the image of his Sig Sauer tucked under the seat.

"Come on, Cooper," the man said. "I'm sure if you think about it, you'll remember me easily enough."

"How do you know my name?" He was now wondering if this was some undercover goon from the government. Maybe he'd be seeing that dark alley sooner than he thought.

"Because I know you," the man said. "I know you very well."

"I have no idea who you are."

When the man smiled, it looked like a grimace. He lowered his head to the opened window and brought his face level with Cooper's.

"You know me," the man said. "I know you do."

"I don't—"

"Think hard." The man's voice was different now. It was thicker, more gruff and raw. His grip on Cooper's shoulder grew tighter when he added: "You know my voice. You know me better than most."

The voice was what did it.

Cooper knew he had heard it before.

The last time he'd heard that voice, it had come from the throat of an eighteen-year-old boy in a hospital bed. That voice had been the only thing in the room until the pastor had come in with his Bible.

"Ah, there it is," the man in the Hawaiian shirt said. His voice was back to normal now, but there was menace in his eyes.

"How?" Cooper asked.

"Easy," the man said with a chuckle. "Do you think we die? Do you think when that insipid preacher expelled me, I ran away into hiding? No. Not at all. I've been following you, Cooper."

"You ran away that night," Cooper spat, trying to ignore the primal fear that was rising up within him. "You retreated at the mere mention of a name."

The man growled, his eyes flickering. He then looked to the purchases in the back of the car. "What are you doing with all of that? Are you sure you want to do what you're planning to do?"

"What concern is it of yours?"

"If you do this, you'll be headed down a road to which there is no end."

"Why do you care?"

"Mind your words," the man said. His voice was still natural and human but Cooper could sense that other thing—the demon —lurking just underneath it. "Just because you think you believe now does not mean you are untouchable. Your faith is small. Puny. Inferior."

"At least I don't wilt and retreat when someone starts reading a book," Cooper said. "Now get your clammy hands off of me. You have no authority here."

He had no real idea what the last comment meant. But he'd heard the preacher say it that night in the hospital room and it seemed to have worked.

The man smiled and released Cooper's shoulder. "I have more authority than you can imagine. You'll see."

Cooper realized the gravity of the situation and knew that the man (or the thing dwelling inside the man) was right. If this was indeed some form of the demon he had watched a pastor expel in a hospital room two years ago, Cooper was well aware that his barely-there faith would not be sufficient to battle it.

He tore his eyes away from the man and stomped on the gas pedal. The car jerked backwards and he pulled hard to the left, pointing the car toward the highway.

"Last warning, Cooper," the man called out across the parking lot. "Don't do this. Save yourself the sorrow."

The old Cooper swam to the surface for a moment and he nearly showed the man a particular finger. But knowing what was driving the stranger made him think better of it. Instead, he didn't even bother looking back in the man's direction. Cooper sped out of the parking lot beneath the bright glare of security lights, making his way back toward the highway.

He pulled out of the Walmart lot and headed back towards Kill Devil Hills. He was shaking from the encounter and, on more than one occasion, he glanced into the rearview mirror, sure that the man in the Hawaiian shirt would be sitting in the back seat. It took a lot to spook Cooper but this had done it. Not once, not twice, but three times he checked the back seat. He could still feel the presence of the thing on him, as if it were trailing him.

Of course, each time he looked, all there was to see was the back window and Jockey's Ridge passing behind him, quiet and still in the early morning darkness.

When he passed by the turn-off that would lead him to the Blackstocks' house, Cooper slowed and looked out to the two houses he had spent time in within the last twelve hours. The lights were still on in the Blackstock home, but Mary's was still dark.

Cooper figured he had another forty-five minutes before the sun came up—maybe an hour at most. If he was going to be successful at what he was planning, he figured he probably needed to get started before sunrise. After what had happened to the Blackstocks in the last few hours, he could only wonder if something similar or even worse had happened at Mary's home. He considered going by to check on her, but he simply didn't have the time.

Behind that, there was the suggestion of the man from the parking lot—a man he was assuming had been possessed simply to taunt him.

Don't do this. Save yourself the sorrow.

The words of that possessed man were far more menacing that Douglass Pickman's demand to go away. And while Cooper's faith might be inferior and barely there at all, he knew enough to recognize that any commands to retreat or give up coming from a demon should be ignored.

That, or there was some trickery involved.

Besides, he knew the demon was, for now, flimsy. If it posed any real threat, it would have showed its power in the parking lot. For now, Cooper knew he had to focus on the caverns and Douglass Pickman.

Driving away from a demon and into the den of a ghost, Cooper thought with a thin smile.

Despite everything he had seen and done in his past, he was pretty sure it had never gotten quite this crazy.

This *hopeless*.

Cooper drove on through the pre-dawn darkness, heading in the direction of Saddleback Campgrounds.

TWENTY-FIVE

I t was still dark when Cooper reached the campgrounds. The road that led onto the property was dark and vacant, showing no signs of life in the early morning darkness. As he crept down the road, he turned his headlights off. The scant trees loomed over him to each side, making it appear a bit darker than it actually was.

He glanced out among the bordering woodland, fully expecting to see the slightly overweight man in the tacky Hawaiian shirt. There was nothing, though—just the slender shapes of trees.

He came to the visitor's center and found the lot empty. Everything was still covered in the murky shades of night that seemed to cling the hardest, sensing that dawn was approaching. Cooper turned left and headed down the same road he'd ventured down yesterday.

Further down the road, he wasn't at all surprised to find that a basic security gate had been drawn closed across the road just beyond the visitor's center. He thought such security measures were a little too much for such simple campgrounds but figured it was better to be safe than sorry, given the often rowdy, young summer crowds. Cooper hadn't thought to look for any sort of gates or security systems when he had been here yesterday. Of course, he'd had no real idea that he would be returning, especially after business hours.

The gate consisted of a pair of simple hinge-operated rails. One sat on either side of the road, their red arms nearly touching three feet above the center of the pavement. Cooper pulled his car all the way over to the side of the road, stopping just before his front bumper kissed the pole that held the left portion of the gate. The car sat slightly lopsided, as the passenger side was nearly in the shallow ditch along the road.

He fished around in his glove compartment until he found a screwdriver. It was part of a small and mostly disorganized toolkit he had thrown in at the last moment before leaving the place he had called home for nearly nine months after returning to civilization. With the screwdriver and his car keys in hand, Cooper walked to the back of the car and popped the trunk. He took out a sturdy hiking backpack and spent the next few minutes doing his best to quickly pack for the task at hand.

He placed three bottles of water in the front compartment of the book bag and then took all of his purchases out of the car. He'd assumed that most of it wasn't going to fit in the bag but was pleased to find that the axe and crowbar fit without much of a fight so long as he left the top portion of the pack unzipped. The head of the axe jutted out as if he were some sort of medieval warrior. As for the sledgehammer and shovel, he was going to have to carry those by hand.

He took the one last remaining item out of the car—the box of salt he had observed nervously before leaving the Walmart parking lot—and placed it in the bag's front pouch along with the waters. He was tempted to open the salt then and there but thought he'd wait until he was sure he'd need it. There was far too much risk of having an accident. If he lost the salt, he might very well be doomed.

That was another precarious thing about being a paranormal

investigator: you often found yourself relying on what seemed like the most trivial and ridiculous things.

He inserted the flashlight batteries into the flashlight and checked it. He aimed a flat white beam of light at the red barriers that sat across the road as a test. Satisfied, he slid the flashlight into the small compartment with the water and zipped it all up.

Finally, he walked to the front of the car and used the screwdriver to remove the license plate. He did the same at the back, working quickly with the weight of his pack seeming to insist that it was time to get going already.

When he was done, Cooper slid the plates down into the backpack where they clanged against the axe handle and the crowbar. If he had left them on the car and someone called for a tow, the plates could easily be tracked when run through the system. They would be registered to Lukas Nye of Salt Lake City, Utah. Mr. Nye, of course, did not exist. He was a creation of the man who had helped Cooper get his footing shortly after he had reappeared. And while his friend's methods were sound and his skills were almost scary, Cooper also knew that a very determined officer of the law would eventually discover where the alias had come from. It just didn't make sense to take such a chance.

The mastermind behind Cooper's labyrinthine bank accounts had also made sure the plates were safe but, he had been quick to point out, the ruse was not bulletproof. Cooper wasn't about to take that chance, either.

Cooper gave the car a quick once-over, making sure he was leaving nothing incriminating behind. He locked the doors and pocketed the keys. He then walked around the security rails and started down the tree-lined pavement that led to the trails. With the bulging pack at his back, tools sticking out form the top, he felt a bit like an old prospector out on the search for gold.

A few minutes into his walk, Cooper heard the first birdsong of the day. The sky had lightened just a bit since he'd parked the car, but he thought dawn was still about twenty or thirty minutes away. Other than the early birds, the only sounds along the road were the gentle clanging of the crowbar and axe in his pack. He carried the sledgehammer and shovel in each hand, both tools propped against his shoulder.

He had walked less than half a mile, but the weight of the tools was already catching up to him. Back in the day, when he had just started as an FBI agent, he'd been a nearly perfect physical specimen; he would have been able to run several miles with all of this weight on him. He'd started his career at exactly six feet tall, weighing one hundred and seventy-five pounds. He'd never really been muscular, but always seemed to have massive reserves of strength hiding somewhere in his just-above-average frame.

But then he had been courted by the seedier undercurrents of the bureau and things had changed—not just physically but mentally. The stress had caught up to him. There had been more travel involved. He'd stopped working out as much and had put on a bit of extra weight. His strength had dwindled as he had replaced a rigorous workout routine with red-eye flights to the next haunted destination or unexplained event.

After he had come back from his disappearance in Tilton, Kansas, Cooper had holed up in a location that only his mastermind friend knew about. He had come back, from that other place he couldn't remember, weakened and slightly ill. After he'd gotten reestablished and found a place to stay, he had done some basic training to build up his frame and endurance. He was nowhere near the chiseled rookie FBI agent he had been twelve years ago, but felt he was of a respectable build for a thirty-six-year-old that had spent the last several years either chasing the unknown or disappearing from the face of the earth.

Carrying the tools on his back and across his shoulder made him think twice about this little self-analyzation, though.

He saw the scattered traces of morning when he reached the first sign along the road. The white embossed letters looked almost like fog on the wooden sign in the scant light of dawn.

A white arrow sat underneath a single word: HIKING.

Cooper took this road, the pavement giving way to dirt. Had it really been less than twenty-four hours since he had driven his car down here? It was hard to believe. It made him feel tired and altogether disconnected. He found himself wondering what Jack Paulson was doing right now.

Probably still sleeping, Cooper thought. *Lucky guy.*

He walked on in the silence of the still and quiet morning. He thought of Stephanie and wondered how long it would be before she reached out to him—*if* she would reach out to him. The scene on the rocks and the eerie connections found in Mary Guthrie's guestbook had frightened her in a way that he had seen before in other people. He was certain Stephanie would come around and accept it all, but he worried about how it might alter her as a person. She could easily become someone very much unlike the woman he currently knew.

And whenever she did process it, she may want to stay as far away from his as possible.

He sort of hated the fact that he wished she was there with him as he huffed it down the dirt road towards the hiking trails. He knew without a doubt that she'd be up for the vigorous exercise but he also knew she'd be complaining in a good-natured way the entire time.

Thinking of her, he checked his phone and saw that it was 5:54. With the knowledge of everything that was ahead of him in the course of the day, his body seemed to ache. When he realized that the day was already passing by with slow agony, a sense of urgency started to broil inside of him.

He started passing signs that boasted familiar names. Echo Trail, Hubbard Trail...and then the one he was looking for.

Pickman's Trail.

He gave the historical marker only a cursory glance. He stopped for a moment and looked down the thin trail that wound away from the main stretch and into the forest. He sat the sledgehammer and the shovel down, readjusted the weight of the pack on his back, and then picked the tools back up.

He started down Pickman's Trail and already felt like he was being watched.

─────────────

WHEN HE REACHED the end of the trail and saw the closed cavern entrance, he set down the sledgehammer and shovel as if they had bitten him. He then shrugged off the backpack and slowly dropped to his knees. The clatter of its contents filled the morning like alien music. He looked down to the tools and thought: *Am I really going to do this?*

Yes he was.

It would be very hard work and he was already doubting the likelihood of success, but yes…he was going to give it a go.

Had there really even been any question? He knew he needed to start now. Any hesitation could cost him dearly. He was going to be making a good amount of noise in the next several minutes and he wanted to be done before the campground workers started milling in…before they spotted an abandoned car without plates parked in front of the gates.

Cooper approached the blockade at the mouth of the cavern and studied it again, trying to find the easiest solution to breaking through. He rolled his eyes at the Do Not Enter signs and the graffiti (*THAT'S WHAT SHE SAID*) as he went back to his tools.

He had no delusions of being able to pry the boards and the plywood supports away from the entrance; the bolts were far too huge for that. They looked to be the industrial kind, not the sort used for projects around the house. Because the boards and plywood were bolted to the rock face, he figured it would be easiest to just try obliterating the boards to the best of his ability, and then prying off what he could with the crowbar.

After all, he wasn't trying to remove the whole blockade. He just needed to break away enough of it to squeeze inside.

He attacked with the axe first, hitting the boards along the edges. The first pop of the axe against the old boards sounded like some strange cartoon sound effect as it filled the forest's otherwise peaceful morning. He withdrew the blade, took aim and swung again, hoping to cause the plywood beneath to splinter. It took a few swings until the boards started cracking, revealing the plywood sheets beneath. The sound was now more like a bomb in the forest as the wood started to give away. The noise echoed in a report that seemed to never end. Cooper had no problem imagining that anyone who might be out for a morning jog along the beach in Kill Devil Hills could hear it.

When there was enough of the chipped and splintered plywood base revealed, he picked up the sledgehammer. He hefted it in his hands and then swung it at the plywood. He got lucky in that the plywood was mostly soft, suggesting either a cheap product or weather damage...or both. Still, soft or not, the noise it made rivaled the commotion the axe had created. Some integral male part of him relished the sound of the destruction as the impact of it rattled his bones and thrummed in his skull.

Within four swings of the sledgehammer, the plywood cracked and started to fall apart at the corners. Behind the broken portion, there was only darkness. Cooper dropped the sledgehammer and took up the crowbar. He attacked the left side of the blockade, where he had already attacked with the axe and sledgehammer. He pried portions away from the rock, some coming off in small pieces no larger than an index card while others splintered off in sections a foot or so long. When he reached the center of the chopped board, the remainder came off in a large chunk that fell to the ground.

When he was done, there was a hole along the side of the blockade that would allow him to slip through easily. He looked at the darkness on the other side and felt suddenly terrified. This alarmed him because, despite all the crazy things he had seen in his time working for the government and traveling as an author of the paranormal, he had *never* feared the dark.

Cooper threw each of his tools through the opening and listened to them fall with a hollow thud in the darkness on the other side. He took a bottle of water from his pack, opened it, and took a few short sips. He wanted to drink more but had no idea how long he would have to make the three bottles last.

He threw the pack on, relishing how light it was without the tools. He heard the flashlight and the other items shifting around as he slid it on, though. Knowing that the flashlight was there made him feel a little more comfortable about going into the cavern, but not much.

Stepping forward, he placed a hand on the partially broken barricade and tried to summon up some sort of vision. What he saw was basically a copy of the scene he had captured yesterday —a tour guide (Jack Paulson) leading a few people down into a relatively creepy attraction. He looked for anything he could find about Douglass Pickman within that hazy vision, but there was nothing.

With no other excuses to delay him, Cooper carefully slid into the opening he had made for himself. He was forced to duck slightly and suck in his gut, but he made it. Inside, with the darkness pressing against him and inviting him deeper inside, the smell of the earth was rich and thick. It seemed to reach up to him like some recently unearthed tentacle, caressing his face.

Cooper looked back out through the opening, into the brightening morning light, hoping he would see it again soon. Then, with a single turn of his head, the world seemed to shift drastically, as there was nothing but darkness to greet him.

TWENTY-SIX

Cooper snapped on his flashlight. A wave of frustration pummeled him like a slap to the face at what he saw.

Roughly eight feet in front of him, there was another barricade, made of the same wood he had just busted through outside.

When he approached it, though, he saw that these boards had been thrown up haphazardly, perhaps as a temporary fix until the much stronger barricade had been placed at the mouth of the cavern. There was no plywood backing here and the bolts were much smaller. He could even see slats of the darkness beyond through cracks along the edges of the boards.

A few hefty swings with the sledgehammer knocked the barrier down, revealing more darkness ahead. His forearms ached with the little bit of force he'd used so far but he ignored it. It was far too early to be feeling any sort of aches. If his hunch was right, his day was going to be impossibly long.

He shone his flashlight forward and saw no further obstructions. What he *did* see was a straight and slightly descending passage with a rock floor that looked as if time itself had polished it to a perfectly flat surface.

The walls were rough and ragged, as was the high ceiling.

Cooper glanced up and saw that the cavern allowed for at least six additional feet above his head. *That's a relief,* he thought. While he wasn't scared of the dark (until about two minutes ago) he did have a slight case of claustrophobia.

He looked back to his tools and wondered if he needed to take all of them just in case. He didn't know how likely it would be that there would be more barriers along the way. Actually, he wasn't sure *what* to expect.

He decided to drag all of the tools a little further into the cavern, just in case someone managed to discover what he had done. He supposed a runner or hiker might see the partially broken barrier at the mouth of the cavern, but what were the chances of them mentioning it to anyone at the visitor's center or the grounds crew?

He didn't know. Honestly, it was the least of his worries.

Cooper put the sledgehammer, axe, and crowbar on the ground after another fifty feet, at a slight bend in the cavern. He kept the shovel in his hand, mainly because it made for a very strange and crude weapon. He didn't want to take any chances and figured he might need *something* in his hands to make himself feel at least modestly secure.

Ahead of him, the passage started to decline a bit more. The flashlight beam revealed the first signs of this place once having been a tourist attraction. There were guardrails bolted into the side of the wall, descending at an angle. There were also metal steps placed strategically to make climbing down the slick cavern floor a bit safer. A small sign had been bolted to the right wall, kindly reminding passersby to *Watch Your Step!*

He walked down the passage, the flashlight beam etching out the cavern ahead of him. There were more stairs, descending down beyond the light's reach. To the sides of the stairs and installed along the lower portions of wall beneath the railings, Cooper could see small lights in the shape of black metal boxes. The protective lenses pointed directly up towards the ceiling, casting up nothing more than dust. Knowing that no light had come out of those things in several years was beyond creepy.

Cooper felt like a ghost that was haunting a location the world had forgotten. The silence within the cavern was eerie. Even the soft shuffling sound of his footsteps on the stairs seemed muffled, as if the cavern walls were absorbing it.

He made it to the bottom of the stairs, where the passage leveled out once again. Here, the floor was a bit rougher than before but the cavern opened up significantly. The rails stopped, allowing about ten feet of open space in each direction. Cooper traced the walls with the flashlight and saw where bored tourists had taken the time to carve their initials into the wall with pens or coins.

With each step he took forward, the passage seemed to grow wider—so wide that it didn't seem like an actual passage anymore, but a small chamber. After another fifty feet, he found himself standing in an area that was even larger, the walls so far apart that he was almost able to forget that he was underground. There were more guardrails bolted into the floor along the right edge. Signs posted at the bottom of the rails read: *Keep Your Children Close!*

The thought of kids being here in this dank, dark place was unnerving. Cooper went to the first rail and saw that it separated the chamber floor from a massive drop-off. He pointed the flashlight down and saw the glittering of countless coins where superstitious tourists had tossed them down for a hopeful wish. The glare of the light made it hard to tell, but Cooper guessed the drop was easily twenty feet.

He continued further into the chamber. Parts of the place looked legitimately interesting. The walls curved in almost sporadic ways, and numerous groupings of stalactites and stalagmites seemed to boast about the secrets the caverns were capable of. The chamber ceiling was textured in multiple ways by centuries of water flow and pressure changes.

Still, despite the openness of the chamber, Cooper found

himself constantly moving the path of the flashlight. The beam of light seemed incredibly thin and almost insignificant when he focused it on a single spot. The darkness down here was impenetrable and had a thick feel to it, like he was walking through some sort of hellish tall grass rather than natural darkness and air.

The silence of the place once again snuck up on him. He felt like he was in some weird primitive isolation chamber. The only thing that broke this sensation was the sight of the metal rails to the left. Cooper walked in that direction and shone the light over one of the guardrails. He saw another drop-off on the other side, this one much shallower than the first he'd seen. He thought this one went down roughly ten feet, although the darkness made it impossible to tell for sure. There were traces of water down there, just enough to make the surface of the floor glimmer and shine in the flashlight beam.

He turned the flashlight to the right and saw more of the same. The guardrails gradually started angling to the right as the chamber started to become more narrow. Further ahead, Cooper could see where the drop-off wound behind a massive outcropping of rock that merged with the cavern wall.

The ocean is that way, he thought.

That made him realize, for the first time, that the campgrounds were over his head. If he could manage to continue walking along the edge of that drop-off in search of a water source, he assumed he'd end up walking beneath the roads and, eventually, the beach.

It would be a long walk, but that was where he needed to go. With the pack on his back, the flashlight in one hand and the shovel in the other, draped over his shoulder, he carried on into the darkness.

Another one hundred feet or so brought him to a severe shift in the terrain. The large chamber took a harsh right turn and started to become narrow again. In the beam of the flashlight, it appeared as if the darkness was actually eating the open space of the chamber. It was a dizzying effect that Cooper had to close his eyes against so he could steady himself.

When he regained his sense of balance, Cooper followed the narrowing chamber into another passage similar to the one near the mouth of the cavern. This one was mostly straight and required no stairs. He came to a curve in the wall as the cavern bent to the left and he saw a copper-colored sign that had been placed along the wall. It resembled one of the historical markers up on the trails, but had a more rustic look to it.

Cooper approached the sign and pointed the flashlight at it. A brief historical account had been engraved into it, reading:

WHEN LOCALS CAME into the cavern searching for Douglass Pickman, they found two coins, a bandana, and a significant amount of blood at this location. There is no way to tell if any of this belonged to Pickman or his daughter, but local legends claim that the blood was still wet.

"CHEERFUL," Cooper said.

His own voice came back to him in what seemed like a thousand whispers. He promptly shut his mouth and vowed to never speak again until he was out of these caverns.

He left the marker behind and carried on. The passage ended a few yards ahead, emptying into another kiva-like area. There were two passages to choose from and he selected the one that had a series of steps directly at the opening. The stairs were incredibly necessary, as the passage went up at a harsh angle and then went instantly down. This passage curved almost the entire way down and, again, came to a much larger chamber.

Cooper didn't know how far he had walked or how far under the earth he was. He estimated that he had been walking for maybe thirty minutes. He assumed that was pretty accurate; he didn't see how any sort of tour guide in their right minds would allow a cavern tour to go on any farther. He tried to imagine Jack

Paulson down here and the thought did absolutely nothing to make the place seem any more comforting.

As if the darkness had read his mind, it revealed a sign against the far cavern wall. It was the only feature Cooper could see. He saw no further passages to take. The caverns had simply dead-ended.

Before he'd allow himself to feel defeated, he shone his light on the sign at the far end of the tunnel. It was just as brief as the one that had come before. In Cooper's opinion, he imagined that this tour had likely not been very much fun, unless you enjoyed creeping around in the bowels of the earth—which he did not.

This sign read:

ONLY A FEW LOCALS *made it beyond this point in their search for Douglass Pickman. Those that searched beyond this chamber were never seen again. It is assumed that they either had a confrontation with Pickman or that the passages beyond were incredibly treacherous and they became trapped.*

THE SIGN INSINUATED that there *were* passages beyond this chamber, but Cooper didn't see any. He slowly traced the flashlight around the room, already furious that he had come all the way down here for nothing. This was the end and he had come up with nothing more than a stark reminder that he did not like narrow places.

But then he saw a slight crease in the wall to his left.

It was about four feet off of the ground and created a dip in the rock wall. Cooper trained the flashlight further up and saw that the wall angled back away from the chamber several feet up, almost to the point that it was perfectly horizontal. It gave the illusion of having created something like a walkway near the ceiling.

He walked towards the area where the slight angle in the

wall started and placed the flashlight there. It rolled back a bit and then stopped when it found the end of the crease. He did the same with the shovel and found that there was just enough space on the ledge to hold it. Cooper then reached up and placed his hands on the ledge, pulling himself up.

With the use of his feet, it wasn't too hard of a climb but it did place considerable strain on his fingers. There was not enough space on the ledge to properly balance himself, so he had to lean forward against the angled wall. Even then, the heels of his shoes were dangling out over the open air. The walkway he had seen from the floor was about two feet over his head and to the right. He could easily get there by spider-walking across the ledge he was currently on.

He reached down very carefully and retrieved his flashlight. It took a bit more effort to get a grip on the shovel without falling back down to the chamber floor, but he managed to pull it off. With each hand filled, he scaled across the ledge. He let out a sigh of relief when it widened after a few steps, making enough room for the entire length of his feet.

After that, getting to the larger ledge further ahead was simple. He threw the flashlight and shovel up onto it and then pulled himself up. It took only the smallest amount of balance and, when he stood up, his head was nearly touching the chamber ceiling. He looked down and realized that, if he fell, he'd likely break his neck. It was probably a thirty-foot drop onto the solid sheet of rock below.

Cooper aimed the flashlight ahead and saw that the makeshift walkway widened out and led into a small opening in the cavern wall up ahead. He cringed when he realized that he was going to have to duck down and crawl in order to get through it.

He allowed himself enough time to take another gulp of water before continuing on. He walked along the top portion of the cavern wall, thankful at least that this ledge was about three feet wide and bordered by the wall to his left.

He approached the small opening and crouched down. The flashlight revealed only blackness ahead.

Cooper slid the shovel inside ahead of him and felt no immediate obstructions. Apparently, this passage was straight and flat. Had it been angled upwards, he had no idea how he'd manage to crawl up it.

With a sigh, he pointed the flashlight ahead and started crawling.

TWENTY-SEVEN

Cooper was immediately relieved when the small passageway not only began to angle downwards, but started to drastically open up in height and width. It took less than five minutes of crawling before he was able to rise up and amble along in a hunched position. Soon after that, he was able to stand. His knees were groaning but he quickly walked the aches out of them.

The sense of isolation along this passage was a complete one; he no longer had the railings or historical markers to break the illusion. The silence was deafening and his eyes seemed to ache for any color other than the earth tones and dark shades all around him. He didn't know if he had ever felt this alone. He tried recalling the memory he had *almost* glimpsed on the beach last night, assuming that, wherever he had been during his disappearance, he'd probably been just as alone. Just the hazy image of that memory did seem to draw up the phantom of feeling, a sense of isolation and despair.

He paused for a moment, taking his phone out of the backpack. Its glow in the cavern was like a weird cosmic light, beaming down to suck him up into another world. The clock on it read 7:12. He'd been in the caverns for a little over an hour now.

The current passage he was walking down was much longer than any of the ones he had passed through along the Pickman's Cavern tour. It seemed to wind on endlessly, not breaking a single time to allow for more tunnels, but opening to chamber length and then narrowing again on numerous occasions.

He wasn't sure how long he'd been walking when he came to the fourth large area along the passage, but he figured it had been at least half a mile. This large opening was bigger than the one at the end of the tour trail with the final historical marker. To the right, the floor made a downward slant and then dropped away. To the left, there were two huge openings, one big enough to drive a bulldozer through.

Cooper carefully approached the drop off to the right and looked down. At first, he saw only darkness below. But when he focused, he could just barely make out faint glimmers of light. He watched the murky movements and realized that he was seeing the faint reflections of his flashlight beam off a body of water. He was sure it was an inaccurate guess, but the water was at least thirty feet below.

The water gave off a stench that seemed to climb the walls of the drop-off and stand directly beside him. It smelled like rotting fish and stagnant salt water. He continued to look down, not sure what he was looking for. He was certainly looking into *dark water* but he felt instantly that this was not where he needed to be.

He then walked over to the two openings. The larger one revealed a rock ceiling that came down at a harsh angle and almost immediately closed the space off. There was another small opening to the right before the tiny room ended. It was a bit larger than the entrance that Cooper had been forced to crawl through earlier.

He aimed his light into it and saw another small room. In the corner, he saw an unexpected shade of white that made him jump back slightly, dropping the flashlight.

He watched the light dance around for a moment before picking it up and once again pointed it into the small room.

There was a skeleton lying against the farthest wall, its skull tilted slightly toward him.

Tattered, moth-eaten clothes clung to its form. It was missing several teeth and its right arm was draped across its chest.

Cooper crawled into the opening and, sure that he would regret it, held a shaky hand out and rested it on the fabric of the shirt. He felt the rib cage beneath and shuddered. He did his best to focus, trying to see if contact with the human remains would summon a vision as he had managed to do at the Blackstocks' door and the boarded entrance to Pickman's Caverns.

It came easily, and quickly—so fast that he let out a cry of alarm. It was as if the skeleton had been holding the memory under its ragged clothes for countless years, ready to give its secrets to anyone that cared. It was sudden, fast, and powerful, making Cooper gasp as it paraded through his head.

He saw a man with long black hair crawling through the large opening outside of this small room. He had a gunshot wound in the stomach, screaming as blood cascaded down his legs. Someone else stood behind him, running away and firing a gun that flashed blindingly in the darkness.

Cooper tried to filter through the vision and settle on the man's thoughts but all he could sense was pain and fury. The pain made the connection that Cooper had gathered a tenuous one, almost like television static in his mind.

He removed his hand from the skeleton when the pain became too prominent. The vision instantly blacked out, bringing the real world back into crystal-clear view. That was fine with Cooper; he didn't need to know anymore. The little bit of information he had gathered was enough.

These were not Pickman's remains.

Cooper supposed it might have been one of the locals that

had come in searching for Pickman, having received a bullet to the stomach for his troubles. Knowing that there was no way to get back to the forests through the caverns with such a wound, the man had apparently elected to hole up in this small opening within the cavern wall to die.

Cooper backed out of the tiny space and walked back into the larger chamber. If there was a way further into the caverns, it was going to be in the second opening along the left side of the chamber. He pointed his flashlight into it and found another small chamber that narrowed into a much smaller cavern.

He took a step towards it and then stopped suddenly.

He'd heard something up ahead.

It had been brief and barely there, but he was certain he had heard it.

A low grumble, like a man grunting or clearing his throat. It came whispering through the opening ahead of him, just barely more noticeable than the sound a breeze would make.

Was it a warning? An invitation?

Or was it just the sound of the earth groaning, complaining about the weight and age it carried?

Cooper didn't know. But he wanted to find out.

With the flashlight beam slicing through the darkness ahead of him, Cooper entered the cavern.

Ahead of him, barely audible but definitely there, he could just make out the low pulsing roar of the ocean.

TWENTY-EIGHT

Cooper had been in the new passage for less than two minutes when he realized that he was now gripping the shovel handle anxiously. His muscles were tense, as if waiting to drop the flashlight and use the shovel like a baseball bat if he needed to. There was nothing particularly frightening about this passage, but it did *feel* different.

Upon entering the tunnel, he had heard the distant drone of the ocean right away. After hearing it, it became all that he was aware of. Underground, it sounded different. It was more mellow and rhythmic than it was in the open air. It was like hearing the world breathing. Cooper wondered if this was what a heartbeat sounded like to a baby in the womb. He stood still for a moment just to take it in and found that it was actually rather eerie.

He walked toward the sound, unsure of how far he had left to go or where he was even going. The sound of the ocean lured him on and he started to wonder.

He wondered if he was under the highway yet.

He wondered how much longer he had to walk.

He wondered if he was losing his damned mind for deciding to go on an ill-advised expedition to explore these uncharted caverns all by himself. He wondered, he wondered, he wondered. It seemed to be all the darkness would allow him to do.

He stopped long enough to take another sip of water and to check the clock on his phone. It was 8:07…still relatively early, but he had no real sense of where the last two hours had gone. To him, it seemed the darkness had swallowed them up. He aimed the flashlight forward and walked on.

Several minutes passed before he realized that the sound of the ocean had grown incredibly loud. He could actually hear the crisp and defined sounds of waves breaking along the shore. As the tide was pulled out, the sound within the cavern walls was like some large beast taking a huge breath underground, somewhere in the spaces ahead of him.

The passage started to descend slightly and then rather dramatically. Cooper nearly lost his footing on two occasions, sparing a spill on his rear end the second time only because he was able to use the shovel as a brace against the floor. His calves were burning and the aches in his knees were starting to become a little more prominent. He'd also started to become much more aware of the dank and dusty smell of the earth all around him and tried not to wonder if this was what a grave smelled like.

He walked down the descending passage and thought he heard someone speaking. It came to him like a whisper. When he stopped to concentrate on it, he was pretty sure it was just some random ambient noise caused by the vast underground spaces and the ocean.

However, less than a minute after hearing the voice-like noises, he felt a slight cramping in his lungs. Slowly, it was getting harder to breathe.

The air felt thicker than ever now and he could smell the acrid stench of the ocean over the other natural earthy smells. He paused, taking in a few deep breaths as he swept the flashlight beam around the passage, making sure he wasn't going to panic and start to hyperventilate.

He took several more steps, now keeping the shovel to the floor in order to support himself, and came to the end of the passage. Instantly, he saw that the rock wall to the right meandered away into the darkness and angled down farther into the earth. He aimed the flashlight down and saw water churning several feet below. Further out, just beyond the reach of the flashlight beam, the water followed the course of a small tunnel. Given the way the water flowed toward it in a rapid, churning stream, Cooper assumed it led to the ocean.

He looked ahead and saw that he was in another chamber, only this one looked different somehow. Everything had a soft golden cast of light to it that didn't need the assistance of the flashlight. Also, there was another absolute ending several yards in front him, barely illuminated by the flashlight beam. To his left, the rock wall curved upwards and to the left before angling back to the right to create a solid wall in front of him.

He cast his eyes up and saw that the ceiling here was fairly high—perhaps thirty feet. He trained his beam of light along the ground in front of him and caught a silver glint in the light just a few steps ahead of him. He walked over to the object on the ground and knelt down to get a closer look.

When he picked the object up, he was rocked by surprise.

He had come full circle. It was almost like meeting himself.

It was the flashlight battery he'd dropped through hole in the side of the black rock two nights ago.

Cooper gripped it tightly in his hand, as if making sure it was real.

He was here. The end of the line.

He could go nowhere else from here except back the way he had come.

Sweeping the flashlight beam upward, he started to understand why everything in the chamber had a golden cast to it. Halfway across the chamber, positioned almost at the very top of the ceiling, was a hole that was roughly the size of a soccer ball. It was the same hole he had dropped the battery down, only a bit wider down here on this side of the thick rock wall. Murky rays of sunlight trickled in through it. Cooper imagined that, during high tide, ocean water would also come in through it, adding to the collected water that filled the drop-off to his right.

He looked back in that direction, getting down on his hands and knees to look into the water. There was a dirty collection of debris and foam floating along the top of most of it. The space between the firm rock on which Cooper was crouched and the wall across from him was roughly twelve feet. Water lapped gently against the far wall, tipped with gritty foam crests. Cooper could see the wall gently angling down into the water until the darkness gobbled it up.

But he also saw something else that made his heart freeze. What he saw did not scare him but seemed to squeeze his heart as a surge of strange emotion surged forward.

He saw three bones scattered along the edge of the wall, pushed and held there by the lazily moving water.

The last bit of bone he saw was a skull. It was hard to tell from the darkness and the limits of the flashlight's power, but he thought he saw others further back into the opening that led back out to the ocean.

He trained the beam of light in that direction and focused. He counted what was at least eight more bones, one of which was a nearly complete right arm connected to a shoulder.

He traced the area slowly with the flashlight beam, coming back towards the lapping water directly across from him. He looked to the first three bones he had spotted and noticed that one of them was clearly a portion of spine. Beneath this broken spine, a fragment of cloth hung, trapped forever to the vertebrae.

The cloth was blue in color. Although it was faded and slightly decayed by time, Cooper could clearly see what it was.

A pair of swim trunks.

From Cooper's vantage point, he could only see a portion of a cartoon shark giving a thumbs-up.

Henry Blackstock.

"Oh my God," Cooper breathed.

In the cavern, his own voice sounded almost evil. A chill crept up his back, then his neck, and then seemed to cover him completely.

He stood up, looking quickly around the room. He glanced around at the water, the light darting back and forth as he searched.

Then he saw something else, but only for a moment. Pressed against the portion of ground that he was standing on, ebbing up and down to the pulse of the water, he saw a body. It wasn't small, per se, but not big, either. It was the body of an older kid, maybe thirteen or so. Its flesh was bloated and white but showed no clear signs of decay.

Kevin Owens.

He'd seen a few dead bodies before, but never a child. And *never* in a situation like this. Cooper took a second to accept the emotion he was feeling—something like sadness, a bit of disgust, and a bit of unexpected anger.

He used his shovel to reach out, intending to push the body away from the side of the cavern floor to get a better look.

From behind him, something grunted.

Cooper wheeled around, nearly losing his balance and falling into the dark water behind him. The cavern grew ice cold and even the ocean seemed to hold its breath as he found himself staring face to face with the thing that he had seen on the black rocks two nights ago.

This time, it was somehow more terrifying now that Cooper knew its name.

Douglass Pickman.

TWENTY-NINE

E ven in the face of absolute terror, Cooper was able to draw everything he knew about the supernatural quickly to the center of his mind. He'd spent most his life learning about the unknown and the unexplained—from an obsession with the Loch Ness Monster at the age of nine to a legitimate scientific study of the Bermuda Triangle as a young adult. In the midst of all that he had learned, there were many facts that instantly came to him, but one was more important than all of the others.

In his current ethereal form, Douglass Pickman could not kill him.

If the specter was powerful enough, it could possibly strike Cooper, perhaps even push him into the water. Depending on the kind of entity Pickman had become over time, he could maybe even *possess* Cooper.

Using all of this knowledge, Cooper was able to block Pickman's first attempted attack. It was predictable and, thankfully, weak. As he had done in the Blackstocks' living room, Pickman tried to force himself into and through Cooper in an attempt to either deplete some of Cooper's mortal energy or to push him into the dark water that had claimed so many lives.

But Cooper was ready for it. As a result, Pickman's form went sailing harmlessly through him. All Cooper felt was a brief sense of being cold, a slight tugging sensation within his stomach, and nothing more. He *felt* rather than heard a slight roar of frustration from Pickman as his spirit began to dwindle.

In the glow of the flashlight, it was easily one of the best examples Cooper had ever seen of a full-bodied apparition disappearing before his eyes. Had he not been so preoccupied with warding it off, it would have been extraordinary.

Why now? Cooper wondered. *Why did he wait to try attacking me now?*

With this thought, Cooper dropped the shovel. He slung his backpack around to his chest and opened the front pouch. He took out the item he had been uneasy about from the moment he'd picked it up from the grocery aisles. Now that he had it in the darkness with him, Cooper thought it might actually save him from further attacks while also getting rid of Douglass Pickman.

He had no idea if his plan would work or not, but it all came down to the blue box he was removing from his book bag.

A simple box of table salt.

As he fumbled with the lid while also trying to hold the flashlight steady, Cooper scanned the remainder of the chamber. Ahead of him, the ground dipped a bit and narrowed. This formation created what was essentially a walkway leading out into more of the water. The further out the walkway went, the walls to both sides pressed outward, allowing more room for the water to collect.

Cooper quickly walked in that direction, well aware that Pickman could choose any moment to draw all of his power together and attack. Out on this narrower ground, even something as slight as a budge in the wrong direction could send Cooper into the water. And while he had no problem swimming (even in water where the remains of countless children resided), he didn't think his plan would work if the salt got wet.

As he neared the end of the rocky terrain, Cooper saw another scattering of bones and the mostly deteriorated fabric of clothes. These were not in the water, but on the rocky surface. The bones were slightly yellowed with age and seemed to be tightly compacted together. There were two bodies here, very close to one another. He saw the stained and faded white cotton of a shirt along with black pants that had a tear in the left leg. Next to this, there was another small pair of black pants and what looked to be some form of a miniature dress.

The reality of what he was seeing came to him right away, along with that bizarre sadness.

Pickman and his daughter, Cooper thought.

Despite the terror Pickman had placed into him, his heart broke at the sight.

He hurried toward the remains, very much aware of how narrow the rocky platform was getting. He had maybe a foot or so of leeway on either side before the stagnant pool of dark water took over.

As he neared the remains, Cooper could feel Pickman drawing near. The air grew heavy with an oppressive weight that wasn't too dissimilar to the feeling of descending in an airplane after a long flight. As his body adjusted to this, he also felt as if there were particles of ice forming on the back of his neck.

"Forget it," Cooper said into the cavern. "Save your energy. I'm not some gullible little child. You won't scare me as easily."

There was another frustrated moan, this one more audible and real than the last. This one was real enough to create a slight echo within the chamber. A small part of Cooper pitied Pickman when he heard the sorrow in it. Yes, he was a frightening ghost but he was, at his ethereal core, still a lost, lonely, and wounded man.

Cooper came to the remains of Pickman and his daughter and dropped to his knees. When he did, he felt something hot along his back, replacing the cold feeling that had engulfed him only seconds before. The sensation was briefly like a bee sting and then throbbed with an icy sort of feeling that he had never experienced before.

Pickman was trying to strike him, trying to shove him away from his earthly remains. He wasn't trying to pass through him or startle him this time; now, he was attempting to attack like a protective father, using fists and fingernails. Using hundreds of years of pent up hate to strike out at him.

Cooper finally pried the box of salt open, ignoring the little triangular flexible spout and tearing the top away altogether. When he did, he felt another stinging sensation on the side of his face.

"I'd suggest you relax," Cooper said. "You won't be here much longer and you should enjoy your last moments. Don't waste them hating me. I've done nothing to you."

Cooper could feel the hate within the chamber like a living, physical thing. It came at him with soft yet tinged barbs of darkness and he again found himself almost feeling sorry for Pickman and all that he had endured. At the same time, though, he could also feel Pickman's presence filling the place, his dead eyes set intently on Cooper.

Cooper leaned to his right and started pouring the salt out onto the ground. As he started making a circle of salt around himself and the remains of Pickman and his daughter, he recalled the first time he had used this approach.

It had been a poltergeist case where a teenager was being thrown from his bed every night. To test a theory, he'd drawn a circle of salt around the boy's bed and had found that the poltergeist was unable to break the circle. Cooper had picked the trick up from an old-school paranormal investigator and had always been fascinated with how such primitive tools could work as well as advanced technological ones. The belief behind the effectiveness of the salt was that it was a pure element of the earth that *un*pure spirits could not encroach upon.

Pickman was apparently aware of what was happening

because he let loose a frustrated wail. Cooper glanced to his right and saw that Pickman's ghost had again re-established itself. It stood just a few feet away in an almost full-bodied form. His rotten face stared at Cooper, his bared teeth a grimace of anguish and eternal hatred. His eyes were hollow, and what served as his ghostly skin was mottled and barely there at all.

Cooper closed the circle of salt behind him, eyeing it to make sure there were no breaks in it. He rattled the box and found that it was a bit less than half full.

"Let me ask you something," Cooper asked as he once again started going through his pack. "All those kids you lured out into the water...all those children you caused to drown...did any of that bring your daughter back?"

The apparition flared for a moment, almost crystal clear and then nearly transparent in the blink of an eye. It came rushing at Cooper but stopped when it hit the circle of salt. It was as if Pickman's ghost had hit some sort of phantom concrete wall. He let out a roar that Cooper felt in his bones. He could actually see some of the salt stir from the force, but the ring around him remained absolute.

Cooper took the box of garbage bags out of the backpack and pulled one out.

"Here's to your health, Pickman," Cooper said.

He reached out and picked up the first bone. He was pretty sure it was a femur. He put it into the bottom of the trash bag and then did the same thing with the next bone. And the next.

Some of the bones had withered so much that they splintered and fell apart at his touch. Yet when he had recovered eight bones and reached the ninth, he felt something like a sharp jolt of electric current pass through him.

His head fogged over and reeled in an unexpected scene that, for a moment, took total control over him.

The vision came with the speed and grace of a fast ball clocking a batter in the shoulder.

Pickman and his daughter (Victoria, Cooper discovered with blinding clarity. *Her name is Victoria) came into the chamber. Victoria was bleeding and gasping for breath. Every breath she took spewed out a thick string of blood from her mouth. Her eyes were vacant, blank.* Pickman was shuddering with anger and fear, not wanting to lose his daughter. He did not care what happened to him. He was only concerned about her. As he sat her down on the floor, looking at the water all around them, he wondered if he should have just given himself up. Maybe if he had handed himself over to the locals—knowing for sure that he'd be thrown into prison or hanged—they could have taken Victoria to a doctor and saved her life.

But instead, his anger had won over and this was where he had ended up. In the dark, with a dying daughter and no hope.

He let out a roar of anger that, before it ended, became a wail of grief. It tore through the cavern, bounding from the walls and carrying across the stagnant water beneath the platform they stood on.

"I just need to rest, Papa," Victoria said. "Please, just let me sleep."

Pickman held her close. His right hand still held his pistol. He could still smell the burning scent of the last shot, the one he put into the guts of one of the locals that had followed him in.

He looked around for any other means of escape, but there was only the water...the dark water that seemed to laugh at him, to let him know that he and his daughter would forever be lost down here. It was so dark that it seemed to merge with the darkness of the cavern walls as the shadows consumed them the further out they stretched.

He listened to the silence and was fairly sure that no one else had followed him.

"I'm sorry, precious," Pickman said in his daughter's ear. He smelled her blood as he kissed her on the cheek.

He felt her breathing softly, a rattle in her chest and something that sounded like mucus in her throat.

She then gave a shudder and expelled her last breath...

...and then sometime later, Pickman held her body close to him. The grief was immeasurable and the hatred he felt towards the men that had so carelessly fired toward her flared through him like a demon. He was starving, he had gone half mad down here, and his sight came and *went. He looked into the dark water and smiled. He leaned over and placed his hand in the stagnant water, making little circles in it. His blood trickled into it, ebbing out like oil.*

"Victoria," he said. "Daddy's here. I'll always be here with you. I'll make them pay, darling. I'll make them pay."

The vision dissipated after that but Cooper thought Pickman's voice rang on for a while.

Cooper remained frozen in place, catching his breath from the force of the vision. He nearly stumbled back into the water but managed to catch himself at the last moment, his heart slamming wildly in his chest. He drew in a deep breath and shuddered. Inexplicably, he found himself on the brink of tears.

He sensed that Pickman had died shortly after uttering that last dark promise to his daughter.

"I'm sorry," Cooper said, his voice low and shaking with emotion. "I truly am. It sucks. It wasn't right. But taking other people's kids is a lame and pointless revenge."

With that, he continued stuffing the bones into the garbage bag. He filled the first one, tied it off, and started on the second. After placing a few bones inside the second bag, he came to the smaller ones.

Another vision came to him, this one timid and without much force.

It was just a blip on the radar, really. Cooper shut his eyes against it and flung the bone into the bag as quickly as he could. He then wiped several tears away. Oddly enough, he didn't want Pickman to see him weeping.

Pickman's recollection had been bad enough. Cooper was pretty sure he'd lost a piece of his soul from just having seen it. He had no interest in seeing Victoria Pickman's last memories of being down here in the dark with her desperate father, in pain and bleeding out.

He sensed a settling of the atmosphere all of a sudden. He knew Pickman was still there, but the ghost had given up.

"I'll take good care of her," Cooper said. "I give you my word."

He wasn't sure what Pickman thought of that comment. His ghost had either exhausted itself or was watching his daughter's remains as they were moved by human hands with a sorrow that extended even beyond the grave.

THIRTY

Cooper didn't hear from Pickman again.

Even when the last of the bones were packed into the second garbage bag to the point that it was hard to tie shut, Cooper was left alone. He knew that there was no way he had gotten every single speck of the remains—both father and daughter—but the ring of salt should serve as a failsafe for anything left behind. Besides, even if the water in the chamber rose to a level that would disrupt the circle (which he doubted, seeing as how the bones had been undisturbed for almost three hundred years), the next step in his plan should take care of it all.

Cooper took a moment to double up the garbage bags, placing the filled ones into another empty one to provide a second layer of safety. He cinched them up and tested their weight. His body seemed to deflate at the thought of the journey ahead of him.

Cooper stepped out of the circle of salt, waiting to see if Pickman had one last fight in him. He gave one final look back to the remains he had seen in the water—the decayed body of Henry Blackstock and the fresh remains of Kevin Owens. He wished he could do something for them, but there was nothing to be done. He didn't have the time or the energy.

He also caught sight of a rib cage further away. It clung to the side of the platform, almost out of sight.

Another body…another kid.

He was tempted to lean down and touch it just to see if he could discover who the kid might be.

Maybe Amy, he thought, recalling the flurry of Scrabble tiles in Mary Guthrie's house.

Maybe it was.

And that speculation was good enough for him. He didn't think he had the energy to endure another vision. Not with the task he had ahead of him.

Cooper gave the remains one last fleeting look and then turned back towards the way he had come in. He started walking into the darkness and couldn't remember ever wanting to see sunlight so badly in his life.

He wore the backpack over both shoulders, gripping a garbage bag in each hand. The bags were flung over the shoulder straps of the backpack. He felt like some deranged Santa, trudging through the dark with bags full of morbid goodies. His shovel was haphazardly tucked into the pack, the spade of it softly nudging the back of his head on occasion. It was not at all comfortable but it was the most sensible way to carry it all.

The garbage bags weren't too heavy…not yet. He had read somewhere that the average human skeleton weighed about fifteen percent of the human's body weight at death. He didn't know if it was true or not, but he kept that nugget at the front of his mind, trying to convince himself that his load wasn't so bad when his arms began to tremble.

He saw evidence of this trembling in the shaking of the flashlight beam ahead of him before he felt it in his muscles. He had to switch the flashlight between hands every few minutes, as it was almost impossible to grip it and the bunched tops of the garbage bags. His wrists were aching within five minutes of leaving the chamber and he had no idea how he was going to get out...*if* he was going to get out.

He did his best to focus on nothing more than the area directly ahead of him. His back started to ache and his wrists were on fire. Sweat was trickling into his eyes and an overwhelming sense of claustrophobia was starting to sink in. The eerie clinking of bones inside the garbage bags wasn't helping at all. A frantic sort of unease started to swirl within him and he did his best to keep it away.

Out of nowhere, he thought of standing in a hospital room, watching a pastor read scripture over a demonically possessed teenager. The pastor had prayed over the boy, asserting authority over the demon, trusting that prayers to God were more powerful than any darkness a fallen world had to offer.

Cooper had always wondered if that was true. While he *did* believe in God (tentatively, anyway) because of that event, the idea of faith and power in prayer was still a bit out there for him.

But as panic slowly drowned him in this darkness, he was willing to try anything.

God, he prayed silently, *I don't know how to do this. Prayer, I mean. I don't even know if you can hear me. So here's the deal: you get me out of here and I'll try to make a point to know you better. I've swept that stirring in the hospital room under the rug like some bad secret. No more, though. Just reach down and help me out of this mess, would you?*

He walked on and then, almost as an afterthought, added: "Oh. And Amen."

With what he was pretty sure was his first prayer ever uttered silently in the darkness, Cooper came to a stop and allowed himself a break. He wasted no time in getting the second bottle of water out of his pack. He took several slow swallows, restraining himself from downing the entire thing. He checked his phone and saw that it was 9:49. He honestly didn't care *when* he made it out, but he'd prefer that it still be daylight. He felt confident that he could make it, but thinking of everything he had left to do made him feel more exhausted than he already was.

Before beginning his walk again, he tried carrying both garbage bags in one hand but it was evident within only a few yards that it wasn't going to work. He was just going to have to carry on with one bag slung over each shoulder. Meanwhile, the shovel continued to ding him in the back of the head every few seconds. On more than one occasion, he wanted to just pitch the flashlight down a tunnel somewhere just to be rid of the extra item he had to carry in his already full hands.

He retraced his steps, doing what he could to slog through the pain. Even when he had just started working for the FBI, when he had been in the absolute best shape of his life, this little hike would have been daunting. His knees were aching, his back was starting to feel like one huge knot of pain, and his wrists were cramping.

He didn't stop again until he came to the passage that had forced him to crawl through when he had entered. Here, he re-checked the knots at the tops of the garbage bags and very carefully pushed them through the tunnel ahead of him. He had to stop twice as the ceiling height dropped. With the black garbage bags in front of him and the ceiling no more than a foot over his crouched body, he felt like he was suffocating. On a few occasions, he felt himself starting to breathe quickly, nearing hyper-ventilating and fighting off what he was sure was a monumental panic attack.

At one point, he stopped, closed his eyes, and shuddered with panic. *How about it God? I know you're up there—I'm pretty sure, anyway. How about it? Get me out of this. I won't offer you any empty promises...I don't even know what to promise. Please...just get me out of this.*

He kept his eyes closed for a while longer, focusing on his breathing and his heart rate. He could feel his heart throughout his body, in the surge of fear through his veins and the frantic pulse in his neck. Once he had control of his breath again, he continued forward, pushing the bags through the tunnel while crawling behind, and ushering the flashlight ahead with his knees.

He then came to the area within the passage that had been easy to traverse coming in—the declining passages that rounded out in curbs in the rock. But now he was having to trudge up them with the bags.

In the dark.

With a variety of aches and pains already tearing through him.

I can't do this, he thought. *It's never going to end.*

Sweat was causing his clothes to stick to him and every muscle in his body was sore. Not only that, but the entire cavern system felt like it was slowly squeezing in, trying to crush him.

I can't do this.

But then he remembered the two bodies he had seen floating in the water in that last chamber, not to mention that last section of rib cage. He saw the bloated skin and that smiling cartoon shark. He saw the countless other remains beyond, victims of Douglass Pickman from the past—victims from God only knew how long ago.

And then he could go on.

And then he *had to* go on.

Cooper came out of the cramped tunnel, pushing the bags out ahead of him and then collapsing on the floor. He lay there on the floor of an abandoned chamber for a moment, fumbling with the book bag and taking more water. He felt like crying but knew that it was not only stupid, but a waste of energy. He took a moment to rejoice in the empty dark space all around him, at the cool, rough rock at his back. He allowed himself a moment to rest, taking a series of deep breaths.

He thought of Stephanie and wondered what she was doing at that very moment. A little ache of sadness passed through him when he realized that even when he was back outside, when he was back in the wide open world and the fresh air, Stephanie would not be there waiting for him.

The thought lulled him, making his head feel light, his eyes weary. It was almost as if the caves were singing him a lullaby.

He thought he might actually be able to fall asleep if he just stayed there, unmoving.

When his legs no longer felt like hot jelly, he checked his phone again. It was 11:06.

Cooper got to his feet, hefted the garbage bags, and pointed his trembling light ahead where the darkness continued to welcome him.

Somewhere further ahead, there was light and fresh air.

And that all the motivation he needed.

It was 11:48 when he came to the area where the Pickman Cavern tour had ended and the more treacherous areas began. He looked down over the ledge to the floor fifteen feet or so below. One garbage bag at a time, he leaned down over the edge and dropped the remains. Each bag rattled like some sick baby's toy. Blessedly, neither of the bags tore or burst open, protected by the second layer of bags he had placed them in.

He made his way down to the bags, pleased to find that it was much easier getting down the ledges and rock wall than it had been to scale it. He wanted to sit there and collect his breath again, but when he saw the gray glimmer of the guardrails and the stairs embedded in the rock floor against his flashlight beam, he forgot about rest.

He was close. Almost there.

He took up the bags and clutched at the flashlight as if his life depended on it.

Cooper continued forward and, when his feet touched the man-made metal stairs that so many tourists had once walked

on, he knew he was going to be okay. His footfalls echoed in the
caverns around him, pushing him forward.

On one single occasion, he thought he felt a slight scratching
sensation along the side of his neck. It was accompanied by a
soft blast of chilly air that seemed to come out of nowhere.

Cooper stopped just to make sure it wasn't his imagination,
He stood on the stairs, listening hard.

"Is that you, Pickman?"

He got no answer. Nor did he wait for one.

Cooper walked forward, his eyes set straight ahead as he
looked for signs of natural light.

———

HE CAME out of Pickman's Caverns at 12:34.

When he saw that the width of the garbage bags weren't
going to fit through the portion of the barricade he had made for
himself, he used the sledgehammer that had been waiting for
him to make the hole a bit wider. Each swing was like a tiny little
spark of flame along his shoulders. His muscles were beyond
spent. As he took the final swing, he vowed to himself that he'd
start working out again when he got out of Kill Devil Hills.

With the barricade opened a bit wider, he was able to push
both bags through. Cooper followed behind them and stepped
out into the forests, instantly sinking down to his knees. He
threw the backpack and the flashlight to the ground and scram-
bled for the water. He left a small amount of the bottle for later,
knowing that his job wasn't done.

He also cursed himself for not buying more. He'd been in such
a hurry that he hadn't properly planned. But beating himself up
about mistakes he'd made almost seven hours ago were useless
now. He had one last thing to do and then this would be over.

Cooper lay down on the ground, listening to the forest. He
could hear no surefire signs of activity anywhere nearby. He

thought he heard the buzzing of a plane's engine somewhere, but that meant nothing to him.

He was exhausted, he was in pain, and there was still an excruciating bit of work left.

I could go to sleep right here, he thought.

But he knew he didn't have time. He got to his feet slowly, picking up the shovel. He tucked it under his right arm and then picked up the garbage bags one last time.

He started walking to his left, into the woods and further away from the visitor's center. He had no idea how the hiking trails wound through the grounds and didn't want to get caught, so he didn't walk very far. When he could no longer see Pickman's Trail behind him and felt safely tucked away by the forest, Cooper set the garbage bags down and took the shovel in his hands.

Before he started digging, he once again listened for any nearby movement. Satisfied that he was alone, he slammed the shovel down into the ground and took up his first shovel of earth.

He then cast it aside and continued digging a grave for Douglass and Victoria Pickman.

THIRTY-ONE

Cooper got back to his motel just after four o'clock that afternoon. He was sore everywhere and there were blisters on his hands from the digging. Several had burst and started bleeding. When he got into the shower, his hands screamed at him as the warm water soaked into his raw, blistered hands. He cursed himself for not buying gloves during his shopping trip. It was just another simple oversight in his hurry to get to the caverns.

He stood under the shower and let the heat work into his muscles. He went over everything in his head, making sure he'd not missed a step. He'd dug the grave about four and a half feet deep. He would have preferred to go six feet but the four and a half had nearly killed him; at one point, he could no longer feel his left shoulder and the world had grown swimmy and tilted. He'd nearly puked at one point as well.

The depth of four and a half feet had been more than enough to contain the garbage bags. Once he'd pushed the bags into the grave, he had poured the remaining salt on and around them. He'd then filled the grave back in, scattering the remaining fill dirt around as best he could. When he was done, he'd scattered woodland debris all around the area, including a partially fallen tree which he'd dragged over. His final act was tossing the shovel deeper into the woods.

The afternoon had been unforgivably hot as he walked directly back to his car where he had barely been able to talk himself out of taking a nap. Luckily, the car was still there, having not been towed. And because he replaced the plates right away, digging them out of his pack and screwing them back on, no one gave him a second glance as he drove out of Saddleback Campgrounds.

Looking back over it all, he couldn't see where he'd missed a step. According to everything he knew and everything he had ever seen in his old line of work, Douglass Pickman should now be gone for good.

Cooper remained in the shower even after washing himself, standing under the hot water until it started to turn cold. He thought of the bodies down in the caverns, floating in that dark water, and wished he could have brought them back. He feared it would be a regret that would haunt him forever.

As grotesque as collecting the bodies might have seemed, Cooper wished he could give the Blackstocks and the Owens at least *some* kind of peace.

Still, he intended to do the best he could in that regard.

WHEN HE KNOCKED ON THE BLACKSTOCKS' front door an hour later, he did so quickly. He eyed the decorative wooden sand dollar, recalling what had happened the last time he had laid a hand on this same door. He was too tired and emotionally drained to go through any sort of vision.

Even if it was something as cheesy as little Henry waving at him with thanks from some mountaintop in the afterlife, Cooper wanted none of it.

Sam Blackstock answered the door. He was dressed in business attire, his tie slightly unknotted and askew. He looked tired and out of sorts. Cooper could relate.

Apparently, though, Cooper looked worse.

Same took one look at him, cringed a bit, and said: "You look like hell."

"Feel sort of like it, too. You guys got a second?"

"Yeah. Come on in. I just got home from work."

Sam led him upstairs to the living room where Cooper sat in the same chair he'd been in two mornings ago, explaining who he was. It felt like it had happened weeks ago. Maybe an entire life ago.

Jenny was standing by the stove, making something for dinner. It smelled like roasted chicken and an assortment of herbs. She waved at him, adjusted the burner, and joined them in the living room.

Cooper got the sense that, even without saying anything, Sam and Jenny knew that he had news. Perhaps he was wearing it on his face, mixed in somewhere among the exhaustion and aches.

"Want a beer or something?" Sam asked.

"No thanks. I just wanted to stop by to let you know that I think your problems are solved. I don't think you'll have any more ghosts in your house."

"What happened?" Jenny asked.

"I found Pickman's remains and buried them properly. His daughter, too."

They both looked shocked at this. Jenny raised a hand to her mouth in either surprise or disbelief. "You...how?"

"I did some exploring. Some caves out near Saddleback Campgrounds. But it's a long story and I'm bone tired."

"Did you..." Sam asked, pausing to make sure he really wanted to ask the next question. "Did you see any other remains?"

"No," Cooper lied.

He could easily recall seeing Henry and the discolored swimming trunks all too well. He simply didn't see the point in putting the Blackstocks through any more pain. The dishonesty did hurt his heart a bit, though.

"Thank you for your help," Jenny said. She looked like she might start crying at any moment, but she looked happy, too. "You're sure this is over?"

"Fairly certain, yes. There *is* one thing I would like to tell you. I don't know if it will help you deal with Henry's death or not, but it couldn't hurt."

"What's that?" Sam asked.

"I believe that the children I communicated with at Mary Guthrie's house—including Kevin Owens—were all victims of Pickman. I know it sounds insane, but all signs point there. I also don't doubt that these were the same children you heard here in your home. The girl you heard was named Amy, by the way."

He watched as an uncertain smile touched Sam's lips and then disappeared.

"I also believe that Pickman had some sort of hold on them," Cooper went on. "He was trapping them there in the dark with him. When you heard them here in your house, they were trying to escape him. I think you heard laughter because they were happy to be away from him, even for a short period of time. In the end, I think he always found out they were gone and took them back."

"Do you think you freed them?" Jenny asked. "The kids, I mean."

Cooper was glad to hear not the slightest hint of doubt in her voice.

"I do. With his remains relocated and properly buried, there should be no sort of hold over them."

The Blackstocks nodded in unison, looking at one another with tears in their eyes.

"So Henry...he's at peace?" Jenny asked.

Cooper had no idea. While he knew that ghosts absolutely

existed and, therefore, cemented his belief in some form of an afterlife, he didn't know what constituted a soul being *at rest*.

But that wasn't what Jenny Blackstock wanted to hear.

"Yes, I think he is," Cooper said.

He hoped it was true.

Jenny nodded, wiped a tear away, and walked back to the stove.

The slight smile of gratitude Cooper saw just before she turned was all he needed. He filed it to his memory, certain that he would need it if he ever hoped to help others in the same way he had helped the Blackstock family.

THIRTY-TWO

After leaving the Blackstocks, Cooper walked down the thin, sand strewn lane to Mary Guthrie's house. When he stepped onto the porch, he noticed an envelope and a small box sitting on the welcome mat.

Written in plain cursive in the center of the envelope was: **Mr. Reid.**

Picking up the envelope from the top of the box, Cooper knew that knocking on the door would be useless. Mary wasn't home. She'd already left for the summer, leaving her house for the coming tourists.

He opened the envelope and withdrew a letter than confirmed this. He stood on Mary's front porch, the ocean whispering to him from behind her house, and read the letter.

MR. REID,

After the events of last night, it became clear to me that there is something larger at work here. Something that I will never fully grasp. It scared me in a way that I was unprepared for. I called the moving company right away and told them I needed to relocate immediately. I am currently watching them pack up the last of my things. I'll be back after the summer, but even then I don't know if I'll stay.

I trust that you have taken care of what you needed to. I saw it on your face while you were here. You looked determined and unafraid. I am so confident that you handled your business and will return unharmed that I have left a gift for you. I hope you might make use of it in the future.

Wherever your journey takes you, I wish you all the best.

Sincerely,

Mary

COOPER TUCKED the letter into his back pocket and picked up the box. He opened it up and smiled when he saw its contents.

He reached inside and took out the small velvet pouch that held Mary's Scrabble tiles.

He turned and headed back for his car but stopped suddenly halfway down the porch steps. He stared out to her driveway, his wiped-out brain trying to process what he was seeing.

The man in the Hawaiian shirt was standing there.

His hands were stuffed into the pockets of his khaki shorts. A lopsided smile was on his face, leering and confident.

Cooper also saw that he was wearing a pair of old battered sandals, something he had not been able to see in the WalMart parking lot fourteen hours ago.

The man smiled at Cooper. "I guess you feel proud of yourself, huh?"

Moving on power and courage that seemed to come from nowhere, Cooper kept walking down the stairs. Honestly, he was also too tired to feel much fear or hesitation.

"No, not proud."

"Then what?" the man asked.

No, Cooper thought. *Not a man. This is a demon...a demon dwelling within a man.*

Ignoring the question, Cooper reached the bottom of the stairs and slowly started walking toward his car.

"How long have you been following me?" Cooper asked.

The man smiled. From that one simple expression, Cooper could tell he'd been wanting to have this conversation for a while. "Since the first time you stepped foot in that hospital room in Virginia," the man replied. "I felt it on you right away. It was hard to miss."

"You felt *what* on me?" Cooper asked.

"The darkness."

"I don't understand."

"I believe it has called you all your life. And when the darkness latches on, there is little you can do to get rid of it."

"If you've been following me for that long, do you know where I went? Where did I go when I disappeared?"

The man shrugged, still standing in front of Cooper's car. "I have no idea. It's…it's out of my reach just as much as it's out of yours. But what I do know is that you have come back a changed man. The darkness is still on you, but there's something different. You believe in our adversary now, which is a shame, but it goes beyond that."

"Why are you here? And what do you want?"

"I warned you earlier. By doing what you did today, you have started something that you cannot undo. And all the prayers and faith in the world won't save you from it."

Cooper thought of the brief prayer he had offered while escaping the caverns and, in doing so, managed to take a few more steps towards the car. The man in the Hawaiian shirt seemed alarmed for the briefest of moments. He stepped slightly away from the car and to the right.

"You did warn me," Cooper said, walking with a bit more confidence now. "But you were unable to stop me. Because you *can't* stop me. Can you?"

"Don't test me, Cooper."

Cooper smiled, despite the pangs of fear that were peeking

out from behind his exhaustion. "You're right, you know? I think I do believe now. And while I have no idea what I'm doing, I know enough. I know you have no authority over me. That's a basic Sunday school lesson."

The man seemed to sense where this was leading. He gave Cooper a mischievous grin and said: "Are you sure this is how you want to play it?"

In response, Cooper filled in the remainder of the space between them. The man took another step back, now unblocking Cooper's path to his car. Standing less than two feet away from the man now, Cooper saw that his eyes were nearly blank and featureless. It looked as if a gray film of smoke was wavering over them.

"It is," Cooper answered. Still frightened but fully aware that he was in control, Cooper walked past the man and opened the door to his car. Then, unable to resist getting in the last jab, Cooper added: "Get behind me, Satan."

The man wheeled around, his face a sheet of hatred. His eyes went from gray to pure black for a moment as Cooper closed the car door. Cooper gave him a little half-hearted salute as he cranked the car.

They locked eyes for a moment and Cooper felt his courage go rushing out of him. He shifted into reverse and left Mary's driveway before the demon could sense it. Cooper's eyes remained on the possessed man until he was out of the driveway and shifting into drive.

The darkness, the man had said. *I believe it has called you all your life.*

Maybe he was right.

But now Cooper knew of other things...he knew that, when he had been at his weakest moment in the cave, he had prayed. And, coincidence or not, it seemed to get him through.

But he knew the darkness was still in him, too.

It was why he was still able to stare the unknown in the face, why he had enjoyed the career that had eventually led him to his disappearance.

Cooper drove off, looking to the velvet pouch that he had tossed into the passenger seat. With the fear slowly vanishing, he made his way directly back to his motel.

Evening was winding down. Restaurant lots were filling with the dinner crowd and he could see the speck-like shapes of people strolling on the beach, enjoying an afternoon by the sea. He watched it all blaze by in a haze, feeling the day's burden weighing him down.

Back in his room, Cooper placed Mary Guthrie's Scrabble tiles on the bedside table and glanced at the clock. It was 6:45.

He was fast asleep before another minute passed.

THIRTY-THREE

H e slept for ten hours, waking up with the clenching roar of hunger in his stomach. As he got dressed, he realized that he hadn't eaten a single thing since the McDonald's drive-thru yesterday morning. Groggily, he packed up his few belongings, intending to check out of the motel and get away from Kill Devil Hills as quickly as possible.

He glanced at the bedside clock and saw that it was 5:12 in the morning. Apparently, it was going to be a while before he got on any sort of regular sleep schedule.

He grabbed his phone on the way out of the room and saw that he had a new email. He opened it up and saw that it was from Stephanie. It made sense that she'd email rather than text. And a call, he supposed, was out of the question for a while. While a text was less personal than a phone call, an email was somewhere far in the distance, way beyond personal.

Her email was short and to the point. It was without sentiment, emotion, or even any sort of salutation. Still, as far as Cooper was concerned, it spoke volumes.

It read: **Worried about you. Reply back to let me know you're okay. Respond via email. Don't try calling.**

Cooper didn't want to over-think it, so he responded right

away with an equally simple message. The blisters from yester-day's work made it difficult to text but he managed with just a few corrected typos.

I'm good. Work done here. On to the next. How are you?

He hoped the vagueness of his message would stir her to send another one. Even if it did, he was sure she'd wait several days to respond. And that was fine with Cooper. It would give him something to look forward to as he tried to figure out where he needed to go next.

After packing up his few things, he went into the main office and checked out of his room. When he pulled out of the lot five minutes later, the scene was eerily similar to the previous morning when he had been taking the steps necessary to break into Pickman's Caverns.

He headed north with no clear reason why. It just seemed like a good idea. He had placed Mary's Scrabble tiles in his car's center console as a reminder of what he had done and what was in store for his future.

Wherever he had been when he disappeared, it had altered him for the better. An egotistical and self-centered Cooper M. Reid had vanished and a transformed, caring (and utterly confused) version had been returned. He had come back with the drive to help others and, so far, he was one for one.

Still, something about the idea of wherever he was brought small twinges of terror to his heart. So maybe the place itself hadn't been particularly pleasant. Maybe it had changed him but in a way he had yet to understand...and maybe never would.

And he was okay with that because he knew he had to be. For now, anyway.

The road unraveled ahead of him, leading him to wherever he felt the need to go. He felt the old Cooper—the pre-disappear-ance Cooper—rile up inside, pumping his fist in celebration. *That's right,* he seemed to be saying. *Let's keep it up. No time to stop.*

There were many things about his old self that he did not like, but he agreed wholeheartedly with this.

But the image of the man in the Hawaiian shirt popped up behind this and grinned at him. Seemingly, the desire to help others was not the only thing that had changed since he had come back.

Cooper drove on as the dawn crept up alongside him. He had no clear idea of where he was going or what he might find himself in the middle of tomorrow, but that didn't matter. Even the approaching dawn, in its slow breach of the night, echoed this.

The road would lead him for now and, along the way, he would do his best to slice open the darkness to let some light spill in.

ABOUT THE AUTHOR

Barry works as a ghostwriter while peddling his own fiction. He is the author of the *It Falls Apart* series and many other genre-breaking titles. He enjoys coffee, ambient music, and irony. He lives in Virginia with his wife and three children.

https://barrynapierauthor.com
https://twitter.com/bnapier
https://www.facebook.com/barry.napier.5

SNEAK PEEK AT BOOK TWO

Here's a sneak peek of Cooper's next adventure in RIVAL BLOOD...

Cooper learns that members of an inner-city gang are dying off in gruesome and mysterious ways. He believes it's the work of a mythological creature that he always believed to be nothing more than the stuff of fiction. As he investigates deeper, he finds himself not only in the middle of a potential gang war, but also hunted by a seemingly unstoppable monster.

Cooper drove by the alley twice before he realized he was in the right place. He'd overlooked it the first time because it looked like every other seedy alley in this part of town. Bordered by an abandoned building on the right and a small laundromat to the left, the alley was a thin and unremarkable space that didn't demand much attention. Even now in the bright light of the early afternoon, it was conveniently hidden by the shadows.

He parked his car in front of the abandoned building. He couldn't tell what the place used to be, and the FOR SALE OR RENT sign in the window had faded long ago. He turned his attention from the building to the alley, feeling uncertain.

There was nothing special about it, nothing to raise any concern. But according to what Cooper had learned, this alley had been blocked off with crime scene tape less than a week ago. The events that transpired in this nondescript alley in the middle of the worst part of downtown Chicago had been covered up and quickly buried.

That was the part of the story that had drawn Cooper's interest more than anything else: that it had been swept under a large, metropolitan rug so quickly.

The murders had certainly been noteworthy, and the nature of the killings had grabbed his attention right away. But the fact that the local PD was trying to brush it aside and that there had been no bureau involvement to this point had sealed the deal.

This is the place, Cooper thought.

Just to be sure, he pulled out his phone and opened his web browser. He had bookmarked the story the moment after he'd read it, pretty sure he'd end up in Chicago to investigate. He opened up the article, not bothering to read it again. He looked at the single picture within the article and saw this exact same alley, only taken at night. Even in the picture, the nearly obscene brightness of the yellow crime scene tape that had been there several days ago looked surreal.

But other than the time of day and the lack of crime scene tape, the resemblance was dead on.

Cooper pocketed his phone and drummed his fingers on the steering wheel. A large part of him hoped that the hunch he had about this place was wrong. He hoped the murders were just random, albeit bizarre, killings—nothing more than the same sort of ritualistic gang violence that had made this part of the city so infamous.

But he knew better.

The evidence was hidden in the two articles he'd read concerning the murder—the one bookmarked on his phone and the second one he'd read the following day. And it wasn't just *this* murder, but similar deaths that had occurred in other locations within a few blocks of where Cooper was currently parked.

He opened the door and stepped out onto the sidewalk. He knew without a doubt that he was in one of the worst parts of the city. That fact alone didn't bother him; during his time with the FBI and the estranged years that had followed, he had been in *much* worse places that this. He eyed the driver's seat of his car, thinking about the gun he concealed beneath it. He hadn't used the Sig Sauer P226 since he had miraculously re-appeared six months ago but old habits die hard.

After all, it did make him feel safer. He hoped he would *never* have to use it again but knew it was a foolish hope.

He decided to leave the gun where it was. He hadn't used it in a while and he knew all too well the trouble a firearm could cause, especially when he was trying to stay off the radar.

He locked the car, pocketed his keys, and looked around as casually as he could. It was just after one o'clock on a Wednesday afternoon. There was very little traffic on the street and the only foot traffic he could see consisted of a grizzled-looking older man sitting under the awning of a pawn shop and two black men in white tank tops talking outside of a small convenience store. The hustle and bustle of big-city lifeblood was several blocks away and may as well be on another planet.

Cooper started down the alley, walking as if he belonged there. He was dressed as plainly as possible, something he had made a point to do that morning. He was wearing a plain gray tee shirt and a pair of pants that hung slightly loose on him. He hated to think in stereotypes, but he knew that the only thing that might seem slightly off about him in this area would be his skin color. This area of Chicago was predominantly made up of African Americans and Latinos. The only white people that lived or did business around here looked nothing like him and he knew it.

Cooper tried to not let this bother him. If all went well, he'd be back in his car in less than five minutes. He looked ahead, further into the alley, and saw nothing of importance. Once the buildings on both side came to an end, wooden slats started running along between them to form a dilapidated fence. Behind the laundromat, there was a single slat that had been knocked away to allow room for a small double-hinged gate. The remnants of a liquor bottle lay strewn about the bottom of the gate in countless fragments of broken glass.

Cooper followed the poorly constructed slats for several feet before the alley came to an end. It ended with a solid wall of more wooden slats where both sides of the alley met. Cooper peered through a small crack in the well-worn boards and saw that there was an open parking lot on the other side. Beyond that, there were more urban businesses, doing their best to hang on.

The alley offered no clues. There was graffiti everywhere, including a juvenile depiction of sex acts and dead policemen. There were several gang markings etched here and there, some of which Cooper recognized from his training with the bureau. There was one for a gang called the Razor Necks and another for the Young Bloods.

He looked at the graffiti for a moment, trying to get a sense of what sort of criminal activity occurred in this part of town. He saw no signs of a presence from any larger gangs—no telltale markings of the Bloods or the Crips.

Stop, he told himself. *You know what you have to do. You know why you came here.*

He sighed and looked to the ground like a kid receiving a lecture.

He saw no signs of blood, no indications that there had been a chalk outline or a thorough investigation of any sort. But none of that mattered right now.

As he studied the cracked concrete, stained with years of rainwater and suspicious foot traffic, Cooper thought of a beach house in Kill Devil Hills, North Carolina. Not too long ago, he had placed his hands on the front door of that house and received his first vision.

He hated to call it a *vision*, but that's what it had been, plain and simple.

It had happened a few times afterwards, too—the most powerful instance having occurred when touching human remains in a cave not too far away from the sea. And while this alley was very different from that cave, the process was very much the same.

Cooper knelt down to one knee, readying himself. He took note of the garbage can by the laundromat wall. If he fell over from the impact of the vision, he'd lean on it for support. The visions were never quite overwhelmingly powerful, but they still took a toll on him. As he considered this, he realized he was a bit scared of what he might see.

Summoning up a bit more courage, he placed his hand to the concrete and focused, willing the vision to come.

It came right away but started out very fuzzy and then thinned out into a dreamlike scene. Cooper saw an African American man running into the alley at night, terrified. His eyes were wide and his face was covered in blood. He kept looking behind him, his breaths coming in ragged, hitching sobs. The man had a gun in his hand but carried it as if he had forgotten it was there. The man reached the end of the alley and—

The vision was broken when Cooper heard footsteps behind him.

He turned quickly and saw three men standing several feet away. They were dressed nearly identical to one another and their black skin was adorned with tattoos.

"This ain't prayer time," one of them said. "And if you ain't praying, there's only one other reason a man would be on his knees in a place like this."

The other two chuckled.

"This is our turf, white boy," one of the others said. "So you better have a good reason for snooping around."

"I—"

"And you can give us that reason," the third said, "right after we beat it out of you."

All three men stepped forward in unison while Cooper was still on his knees. From his vantage point, the first thing Cooper became aware of was the gun tucked into the waist of the leader's pants.

Cooper suddenly felt very stupid for leaving his own gun in the car. But there was no time to chastise himself. Now, he had to figure out how to stay alive in this suddenly grim situation.

Afraid to stand up or to even say much of anything, he could only hope for the smallest of openings as the three armed men continued forward.